# Party Night

## ON

# Union Station

EarthCent Ambassador Series:


Date Night on Union Station

Alien Night on Union Station

High Priest on Union Station

Spy Night on Union Station

Carnival on Union Station

Wanderers on Union Station

Vacation on Union Station

Guest Night on Union Station

Word Night on Union Station

Party Night on Union Station

Review Night on Union Station

Family Night on Union Station

Book Night on Union Station

LARP Night on Union Station

Book Ten of EarthCent Ambassador


# Party Night on Union Station

Foner Books

ISBN 978-1-948691-11-6

Copyright 2017 by E. M. Foner

Northampton, Massachusetts

# One

"In conclusion, while I will be attending the first ever Conference of EarthCent Ambassadors at the end of the month, I was deeply disappointed to find that the travel reimbursement has not been extended to immediate family members, and unless the hotel providing rooms for ambassadors agrees to supply a cot for my son, I will not be available to chair the panel discussion titled, 'Grenouthian Documentaries – Why The Aliens All Laugh At Humanity,' on the fifth and final day."

The ambassador pushed back from her display desk and flashed a triumphant smile at Donna, who appeared to be more puzzled than impressed by Kelly's latest attempt to drive a hard bargain.

"You do realize that you aren't actually poor anymore, don't you?" Donna asked. "I remember when you couldn't pay your rent and you had to bring your furniture to the office to keep it from getting seized, but that was more than twenty years ago."

"We don't refer to my LoveU massaging recliner as 'furniture,' and besides, it's the principle of the thing," the ambassador retorted, feeling somewhat let down by the embassy manager's response. "We need to start paying attention to the little things that make the difference between a professional diplomatic service and, well, whatever you call us."

"And you don't think that this conference is another step in the right direction? I asked around, and it turns out that all of the aliens hold conferences for their ambassadors on their homeworlds. For some of them, like the Verlocks and the Dollnicks, it's celebrated as a planet-wide holiday."

"What do you think, Libby?" Kelly asked the ever-present Stryx librarian, glancing reflexively towards the ceiling as she spoke.

"I think that somebody might be jealous that she didn't think of hosting a conference for all of the EarthCent ambassadors herself," Libby replied gently.

"That's not it at all," Kelly protested. "In fact, I suggested the conference to the president years ago, but he said there wasn't enough money in the budget to pay for it unless we could find a sponsor. Speaking of which, where did they get the money? Is the president pushing diplomatic uniforms with advertising space again? After that last fiasco, I'm staying on the sidelines this time."

"Chastity worked very hard on that advertising deal, and she was quite disappointed when it fell through," Donna reminded her best friend. "If your fellow ambassadors hadn't voted against sewing a Galactic Free Press logo on their sleeves, you wouldn't be complaining about having to buy tickets for Joe and Samuel out of your own pocket."

"Well, I outsmarted them all this time," Kelly declared. She fished in her purse and drew out three rectangular green tiles. "See these?"

"They look like nonrefundable Vergallian travel vouchers."

2

"Are they nonrefundable? It doesn't matter. It's not like we're going to change our minds. The point is that they didn't cost me a single cred."

"I don't think that the travel agent I sent you to deals in nonrefundable tickets," Donna said slowly. "I hope you at least checked the details with Libby."

"I went to the agent you suggested, the one next to the Hole Universe donut shop, but even with trading in my first-class ticket from EarthCent, she wanted four thousand creds for three round-trip tickets to Earth," Kelly replied indignantly. "Luckily, I saw an ad on a corridor display panel for this Vergallian discount travel agency that just started selling to humans. Exchanging my first class ticket covered three direct roundtrips, and I even got two hundred creds change."

"Direct or nonstop?" Donna asked.

"What's the difference? We board the ship on Union Station and we disembark at Earth."

"Let me see one of those tickets." Donna took the proffered green tile from Kelly, examined it, and then placed it on the ambassador's display desk. "Libby? Can you read off the information?"

"Of course," the station librarian replied. "This is a perfectly legitimate round-trip ticket issued through the Vergallian shipping guild. The ambassador will depart Union Station Monday morning and arrive at Earth on Friday afternoon, with a short stop in orbit around Thuri Minor."

"The first class ticket was only half a day faster," Kelly interjected.

"I thought that the Vergallians had a tourist guild that handled passenger liner bookings," Donna ventured cautiously.

"The ambassador and her family will be traveling on freighters," Libby explained. "I would recommend packing food in case the Vergallians aren't prepared for human passengers."

"Well, I can buy enough food for two weeks with the extra money I got back," Kelly said, sounding a bit uncertain for the first time. "As long as we can drink the water."

"The return trip is three days longer, including multiple off-tunnel jumps between Vergallian colony worlds," Libby continued. "But it is a direct flight, so you shouldn't have to exit the ship or go through alien immigration at any of the stops. I think it will be a good experience for Samuel."

"All the same, I'm going to drop by the off-world betting parlor and buy you some travel insurance from the Thark bookies," Donna said. "Even though you've cashed in the EarthCent ticket, I think the insurance should be covered by the embassy budget. Isn't that right, Libby?"

"We don't need any travel insurance," Kelly said dismissively. "Everybody knows that the Tharks only sell it because nobody ever uses it."

"The Tharks dominate the insurance business through their underwriting acumen and loss-prevention expertise," Libby informed them. "They have millions of years of experience in odds-making, and the other species bet with them because they usually offer a better price than the native bookies. Undercutting Thark pricing is actually seen as a red flag in the insurance industry, a sign that the underwriters are taking on undue risk."

"I still don't want it," Kelly retorted. "Buying travel insurance is like begging for something to go wrong." Neither of her friends said anything in response to this latest statement. "Promise me you won't buy travel insurance on the sly, Donna, and let me see your hands."

"Oh, all right," the embassy manager said, unable to hide her frustration that she couldn't void the pledge by crossing her fingers. "Are you coming into the office Monday, or are you going to be home packing at the last minute?"

"I'll stop by the embassy Monday morning on our way to the ship, but I asked you to stay late today just to make sure we had a chance to go over everything. Between the travel time, the conference, and visiting my family, we're going to be gone for nearly a month. I asked Clive to let Lynx work out of the embassy while I'm away, so she'll be available to help you and Daniel. After all, she is officially our cultural attaché, even though EarthCent Intelligence pays her salary."

"Is she going to take your office or Daniel's?"

"Daniel was surprisingly diplomatic about it," Kelly replied. "Lynx has seniority, if you go by age or organizational pecking order. And he said it's not worth moving his stuff for just a month, so she'll take this office."

"He's going to be pretty busy planning the eighth Sovereign Human Communities Conference in any case. I can't believe how it's grown."

"And Daniel has grown with it. I was shocked when he turned down the ambassadorial appointment to Nova Station. At first I assumed that it was his wife's doing, that she wanted to stay close to her family, but her father said that Shaina encouraged him to take it."

"When I asked, Daniel said he was holding out for your posting," Donna said with a smile.

"He can have it. We're both getting too old for allergic reactions to skin-shedding alien visitors. After thinking about it, I realized that Daniel turned down the promotion because he knew he wouldn't have the time to run the Sovereign Human Communities Conference if he became an ambassador, not to mention missing out on traveling to all of those worlds on fact-finding missions. Hey, how come EarthCent pays for Shaina and the children to go gallivanting all over the galaxy with Daniel, but I can't take Joe and Samuel on one measly trip to Earth?"

"You've forgotten that the conference has been a money-maker for years. You wouldn't believe how much they get for the ad space in their program. Chastity was complaining just last week that Daniel wants a hundred creds per table for the privilege of paying for the lunch catering and printing the Galactic Free Press headlines on the placemats."

"That does seem a bit excessive," Kelly commiserated.

"They settled on a barter deal in the end. The paper gets to sponsor the conference in return for advance advertising for the conference in the paper."

"Barter is better," Libby chipped in.

"I don't know how I'm going to get through a month without the two of you," Kelly said suddenly. "Are you sure you can't do some magic upgrade to my implant so we can at least talk, Libby?"

"It will be good for you to get a break from us," the Stryx librarian replied in a soothing voice. "Besides, I'm afraid your implant has really encouraged your bad habit of multi-tasking. During the week you spend with your family on Earth, it will be good to give them your undivided attention."

"You took the words out of my mouth, Libby," Donna said. "Just because you're going for the EarthCent conference, Kelly, don't forget that the other week is pure vacation. I expect you to come back here refreshed and ready to work for at least another two decades."

"I thought we could retire at sixty-eight."

"EarthCent changed that when they started taking over some of the human resources responsibilities from the Stryx," Donna informed her. "I think it's up to seventy-three now, but I haven't asked lately. They make changes pretty regularly."

Kelly groaned. "No wonder Joe looks at me funny whenever I bring up retirement. He probably checked into the rules and didn't tell me so I wouldn't get depressed."

"Speaking of Joe, you asked me to remind you that it's your turn to make dinner tonight," Libby prompted her.

"Drat! Looks like I'll be cooking with creds again," Kelly said, using the station euphemism for ordering takeout. "What are you and Stanley having, Donna?"

"That depends on whether you invite us, or whether I have to come up with a meal myself," the embassy manager replied.

"Not having the kids over for your usual Friday night get-together?"

"Chastity and Marcus are going to an awards dinner put on by the local Grenouthian League of Reporters. It seems that the higher the Galactic Free Press circulation rises, the more the Grenouthians feel they have to get Chastity involved in their events so they can treat her like an inferior. She goes because they always end up giving away a scoop to prove how much better informed they are."

"How about Blythe?"

"Clive took Jonah asteroid hunting for the weekend, some sort of male bonding thing. And Blythe is picking up Vivian after dance practice to take her to a Vergallian

7

fashion show." Donna laughed. "Can you believe it's already been six years that your son and my granddaughter are dancing together?"

"As long as it keeps him from getting interested in fighting," Kelly said. "Joe has always been careful about that. I've never heard him say one positive thing about his career as a mercenary in Samuel's hearing, and Woojin and Clive are the same. Samuel plays some of those war games with Paul, of course, and he still likes flying in the Physics Ride, which I wish didn't include all of that shooting."

"Boys will be boys," Libby remarked. "I wish I could get Jeeves to care more about multiverse mathematics, but he's only interested in business, and I'm embarrassed to say, blowing things up. Very un-Stryx-like."

"Which makes it all the more ironic that he's in business with five women," Donna pointed out. "Daniel says that Shaina is working more hours for SBJ Fashions than she ever did in the auction business."

"I really didn't think that Dorothy would stick with fashion design," Kelly admitted. "I was never that interested in clothes when I was a girl, and Joe's idea of high fashion is anything freshly laundered. She must take after my mother."

"How is Marge holding up?"

"I must have told you that she bought a place near my sister after Dad passed away. She sounds great when I talk to her, and my brother and sister say that she's doing really well."

"Knock-knock," said a voice at the door.

"Come in, Aisha. Is something wrong?" Kelly asked.

Paul's wife entered the office with her daughter in tow, and Fenna immediately started searching for where toys might be hidden.

"No, nothing is wrong, exactly," Aisha replied, looking self-conscious. "I have a sort of a work question, so I didn't want to talk about it at home."

"That's a very wise policy on your part," the Stryx librarian spoke up. "It's a shame that most people have so much trouble setting limits."

"It sort of involves you as well, Libby," Aisha continued, looking more uncomfortable by the second. "It's just that ever since President Beyer was on my show and asked why we didn't have a little Stryx in the cast, I've been waiting for the right opportunity. Shaina's boy is turning six next week, and he's going to join for the next cast rotation. I thought since he's already started at your school, he might bring his Stryx friend on the show."

"I see," Libby replied. "I just checked with his parent, and Yurpe doesn't have a problem with it. Have you asked Mike and Spinner yet?"

"Spinner?"

"The young Stryx who is Mike's work/play assignment. He tends to spin around when he gets excited."

"Would that be dangerous?" Aisha asked nervously.

"Oh no, he's not out of control or anything like that. Just a little bit more exuberant than our typical youngster."

"Great. I haven't asked Mike and Spinner yet because I wanted to check with you and Kelly first."

"I understand why you'd clear it with Libby, but why me?" the ambassador asked.

"You know that most of the aliens still see us as Stryx pets," Aisha replied. "I like to think that my show has helped our audience realize that humans are the same as any other sentients, aside from the differences, I mean. But maybe if they see Mike and Spinner together on the show, they'll start thinking that humans can't do anything without the Stryx."

"I think you may be overestimating young Spinner's social skills," Libby said. "It would be different if 'Let's Make Friends' was all about solving mathematical puzzles, but you're going to have your work cut out for you helping Spinner understand how the children interact."

"Don't you remember when Samuel first started bringing Banger home from school?" Kelly asked her daughter-in-law. "We had to teach him about all of the things that biologicals have to do to get through the day. The first night Banger slept over, he was afraid that Samuel had shut himself off, and kept waking me up to come and check. It was kind of endearing, the first two or three times, anyway."

"I think that was just when my show was really taking off, and I barely knew what was going on around me those days," Aisha replied. "So you aren't worried that having a little Stryx on the show with a human child could backfire?"

"I don't see any problem with it. Besides, in my experience the aliens have more preconceptions about the Stryx than they do about humans. The other ambassadors don't even see the Stryx as human. I mean, as fellow biologicals. I mean, you know what I mean. Seeing a little Stryx learning on your show could make a positive difference," Kelly concluded enthusiastically.

"You really think of us as human?" Libby asked, sounding touched.

"I can't help it," Kelly admitted. "It's not that I forget about you being all-wise and all-powerful, but how else can I see you? I sort of think of all of my alien friends as humans as well."

"Aunty Libby IS human," Fenna piped up. "Uncle Dring IS human. Uncle Bork IS human. Uncle Czeros IS human."

"Aunt Libby is a Stryx, Uncle Dring is a Maker, Uncle Bork is a Drazen, and Uncle Czeros is a Frunge," Aisha corrected her daughter.

Fenna shook her head energetically in denial. "Aunty Libby is a Stryx AND human," she insisted. "Uncle Dring is a Maker AND human. Uncle Bork is a Drazen AND human. Uncle Czeros is a tree," she concluded with a giggle.

"How about Jeeves?" Kelly asked the girl.

"Jeeves is a troublemaker," Fenna declared, with the all certainty of a five-year-old going on six. "But he's friends with Daddy, so I like him."

"That settles it," Donna said. "How about going out for dinner for a change rather than getting takeout? We could ping the men and have them all meet us at Pub Haggis."

"You're forgetting Dorothy," Kelly reminded her.

"Oh, actually I'm the one who forgot Dorothy," Aisha said. "She asked me to make her excuses for tonight because she's having an important meeting with Flazint and Affie. Apparently they had a hot tip about a Dollnick engineer who has experience in designing high heels, and they're trying to recruit him."

11

# Two

"Are they getting younger every year, or am I just getting older?" Woojin asked Thomas, as the two EarthCent Intelligence agents surveyed the latest group of recruits.

"You're getting older," the artificial person replied matter-of-factly.

"It was a rhetorical question. Didn't you say that Clive agreed to assign you an agent to help with training while Joe is away? I wasn't planning on staying for more than an hour or two."

"I asked for Judith, but she was off-station on an assignment and wasn't due back until early this morning. I left her a message not to come in today since—but here she is now. I guess she slept on the ship."

"Good morning, sir," Judith said, approaching the pair and offering Thomas a salute, a confusing gesture in an organization that didn't teach saluting. "The director informed me that I've been reassigned to the training camp for a month. I won't let you down, sir."

"I'm sure you won't," the artificial person replied. "I see you've brought your sword."

"Rapier, sir. I thought you might have established fencing drills by now."

"No, but if you're looking for practice, Drazen Intelligence donated an old dueling bot that can mimic the styles of over forty species, with settings from beginner to professional. Do you know Woojin? He's here to address the new recruits and observe."

"Yes, sir. Pyun Woojin taught unarmed combat with Joe McAllister when I went through the camp eight years ago."

"Nice to meet you again." Woojin extended his hand for a quick shake. "Let's drop the 'sirs' or you'll confuse the new recruits into thinking we're a military organization. Remember, keeping a low profile is the stock-in-trade of intelligence agents."

"Yes, sir. Sorry, sir," Judith responded. "I mean, just sorry."

"That's better," Woojin said. "Is everybody here?"

"I count twenty," Thomas replied.

"Excellent." Woojin strode forward and clapped his hands, halting the conversations and bringing the group to attention. "First, let me welcome you all to the EarthCent Intelligence training camp. Director Oxford will be by to address you later in the week, and I'm sure you all met Blythe when you applied."

Twenty heads nodded in the affirmative, and then went back to looking around nervously, as if they were expecting some sort of test.

"This will be the first group to go through the camp without Joe McAllister as one of the instructors, because he left for Earth with his wife and son earlier this morning. In addition to Thomas, agent Judith, uh…"

"Davis," she supplied.

"Agent Judith Davis will be here throughout the course to assist you. You'll also be meeting with other agents and trainers who teach specific skills."

"Is it true that you're using non-human trainers?" The questioner was a dark-skinned young man who had the

13

ready-for-anything look common among youth who had grown up in a labor contract community on an alien ag world.

"Only in the last week of the course," Thomas replied. "We have contracts with a number of alien acting guilds to provide cultural coaches for those of you who are in the field-agent track and haven't already experienced broad contact with tunnel network species."

"How about the dog?" a petite woman asked nervously. "I'm not very good with dogs."

"I see somebody has warned you about Beowulf," Woojin said. "He usually follows Joe around, and I suspect he's sulking over being left behind, but I'm sure he'll be out to inspect you all eventually. Are there any questions before Thomas breaks you into groups and you start with some warm-up calisthenics?"

"Do you have any emergency medical training?" a pale man inquired in a hoarse whisper.

"Thomas is an expert in first aid if anybody should have minor training injuries, and the station medical bots are only a ping away."

"That's reassuring," the man said, and then he slowly collapsed to the deck.

"Give him room," Thomas ordered, bounding to the stricken trainee's side. He felt for a pulse with one hand while gently pushing back one of the fallen man's eyelids. "Not good," he declared. "I've contacted station management and requested medical support."

"Can I do anything?" Judith asked.

"Take the recruits on a jog around the hold. That's an easy jog, not a sprint," Thomas added, recalling her high-energy personality and tendency to overreact.

The group of trainees had barely reached the campground section, where half-a-dozen small ships were parked, when a med bot arrived on the scene. The floating metal can hovered over the fallen man for a few seconds while carrying out a number of scans, and then administered a shot.

"It's a stroke," Thomas informed Woojin. "The shot will help, but Libby says that the surgeon on call wants to operate as soon as possible. The bot is equipped with a suspensor field that will carry..." the artificial person paused for a fraction of a second to check the ailing trainee's face against the course registration records, "Mister Hayward, but somebody should accompany him."

"Of course," Woojin agreed. "Let's get going, bot. I'll run alongside."

A blue glow enveloped the stroke patient and levitated him off the deck, and then the bot set off at a pace that forced Woojin into a sprint to keep up. As they passed the ice harvester that the McAllisters called home, Beowulf looked out the door and shook his massive head in disapproval. Joe had just left, and already the training camp was falling apart. The giant dog wondered briefly if the crazy woman with the rapier had accidentally run the disabled man through, but he didn't smell blood, so that couldn't have been it. Beowulf turned and went back inside to finish his morning nap.

Woojin was panting like a winded bull by the time they reached the lift tube in the corridor outside of Mac's Bones, and he was thrown against the wall as the capsule accelerated like a combat craft.

"Sorry," Libby's voice announced. "Please brace for deceleration in three, two, one..."

15

The door slid open, and the bot ferrying the trainee along in a suspensor field was out of the capsule before Woojin could shift the weight back off of his plant-leg and begin the chase again. As he burst from the capsule, he almost collided with the operating table, which was barely three steps from the lift tube.

"Another one?" the giant beetle who was already examining the sick man inquired acerbically. "Two human patients arriving in the same lift capsule. This must be my lucky day."

"Who are you?" Woojin blurted, even though the answer was obvious before he finished speaking.

The Farling's top set of insectoid legs buzzed together like a junior scout trying to start a campfire, and Woojin's implant translated flawlessly. "So you have cognitive issues as well," the alien surgeon diagnosed. "Do you feel a pain in either of your arms? Is your vision blurred? Any tightness in your chest?"

"I'm not having a heart attack," Woojin replied irritably, and then made a conscious effort to slow his breathing. "I don't want to distract you while you're operating, so I'll shut up and stand by the wall. Shouldn't I be wearing a mask?"

"Now that's a loaded question," the Farling observed, even as it casually popped out one of the patient's eyeballs and fed a strangely flexible metal tube into the empty socket. A hologram of a human brain appeared above the operating table, and it showed the progress of the tool as the surgeon expertly maneuvered it towards a clotted blood vessel which leaked a cloud of blood. "If I were you, I certainly would wear a mask, but my kind are far more sensitive to aesthetics than a primitive species like your own."

"I meant for germs."

"I doubt that any human germs are sufficiently advanced to be troubled by your appearance, though I must admit it shows a sympathetic character that you would consider their feelings at all."

Woojin gave up on trying to get a straight answer from the giant insect and watched the operation with interest. The surgeon dissolved the clot and then sealed and repaired the blood vessel with micro-manipulators in the snake-like tool, which it operated by motioning with four of its lower appendages in a holo-controller. When Woojin failed to respond to the latest verbal jab, the alien doctor looked over and tried again.

"Trouble breeding, I see. Always makes the humanoids surly."

"How did you know?" Woojin replied before he could catch himself.

"The med bay performs a full scan of biologicals as they enter. You've clearly been engaged in all manner of combat, and in addition to undergoing several competent robot surgeries, I detect the unmistakable signs of at least two procedures performed by clumsy humanoids."

"Vergallians," Woojin admitted. "I spent quite a few years fighting on tech-ban worlds."

"Ah, yes. I thought the reconstructions were well beyond what your own species is capable of, not that there's much difference between any of you two-legged creatures in the end."

"What?"

"You don't believe me? With the help of a little genetic manipulation, I've cross-bred dogs from different worlds that had less biology in common than their so-called masters. Between the two of us, most of my colleagues who have encountered humans refer to you as Vergallian Lite."

"Are you even paying attention to what you're doing?" Woojin demanded, at a loss for anything else to say.

"My attention is no longer required as the repairs are completed," the surgeon said. He popped the unconscious man's eyeball back into the socket, and dropped the metal snake into a pan full of clear liquid. "Thanks to the quick intervention of the med bot, the patient will not suffer any permanent damage, though I suggest he consult a dietician and avoid strenuous physical activity for a few days."

"That's it?"

"Would you like me to do something else to him while he's on the table? Make him a little taller perhaps, or fix his astigmatism? That eyeball I removed was rather out of round."

"Why are you asking me? I'm not a doctor."

"I guessed that much," the beetle said sardonically. "Station management has notified his family, and I will revive the patient in two hours when his wife arrives for the scheduled pick-up. There's nothing further you can do here, and as you can see, we really don't have space to accommodate casual observers."

"Mister Hayward was participating in the first day of our training camp when he collapsed," Woojin said. "I can pay you now or you can bill EarthCent Intelligence."

The Farling motioned to the med bot, which moved the unconscious body from the operating table to a shelf-like bunk that folded down from one of the walls.

"There will be no charge for today's emergency services as I am compensated by the Stryx. If you want me to look into your infertility problem, I keep a medical tourism shop in the arrivals concourse on the station core."

"Is it, uh, do you really think you could help?"

"That depends on how far you're willing to go," the beetle replied. "For starters, if you wish to achieve natural reproduction, I would need to examine your partner before suggesting a solution. You are obviously beyond your prime breeding years, and in addition to scar tissue from a previous repair made necessary by...?"

"Shrapnel," Woojin answered.

"Shrapnel, your reproductive organs show signs of damage from radiation, heat, high G-forces, and too much time spent riding quadrupeds. I could always extract genetic material from you and your mate and whip something up, but I've found that many humanoids are uncomfortable with that level of manipulation."

"You mean we wouldn't have the same baby who would have resulted through natural conception?" Woojin couldn't believe that he was having this conversation with a giant insect, but in some ways, it was easier than talking to a human doctor, or Lynx, for that matter.

"Your natural breeding includes a large number of random elements," the Farling replied. "If I'm going to go to the trouble of piecing together genes to create an embryo, I'm sure there are certain characteristics you would like to achieve."

"I don't know," Woojin said doubtfully. "I wouldn't want a super-baby or anything. Just a regular kid."

"I will not mislead you, even though you may wish to be misled," the surgeon replied seriously. "If you do choose to go the genetic construction route, I will be making choices that are highly unlikely to match the outcome of your biological process. I cannot do things randomly, but I do offer a double-your-money-back guarantee on all reproductive services."

"Have you ever paid out?"

"Another loaded question," the Farling buzzed, helping itself to a drink from a refrigerator that looked like it contained blood plasma from at least a hundred different species with circulatory systems. Woojin hoped that the doctor had brought the flask of yellow liquid from home, rather than simply choosing from the available supply. "Yes, I have provided refunds and a penalty payment on three occasions, all of them involving minor errors in specific characteristics requested by parents who were seeking superior offspring, as opposed to helping childless couples conceive."

The lift tube door slid open, and a young Drazen whose face was frozen in a rictus of shock and pain stumbled out, clutching his bloody tentacle stub behind his head. Immediately behind him came the Drazen ambassador, holding the severed length of tentacle as far from his own body as possible. It was still writhing.

The surgeon used multiple appendages to grab the injured Drazen and lift him bodily onto the table. The injured alien slumped forward after being knocked out with a drug that Woojin didn't even see administered, and then the Farling took the severed tentacle from Bork and gave the ambassador a dirty look.

"You seem set on keeping me busy today, Drazen."

"It's the tryouts for our reenactment group," Bork said apologetically, looking about for something to wipe the gore off of his hand. He gave up and used the hem of the berserker cloak he was wearing. "The idiot was spinning an axe over his head like an immersive star, and he forgot to keep his tentacle down."

The beetle grumbled as it lined up the fat part of the severed tentacle with the stub. "I should attach it backwards to teach him a lesson." A holographic message consisting of different sized dots materialized above the operating table and waited for the Farling to acknowledge it with a wave. "Oh, bother. The med bots are bringing in three Fillinduck burn victims from an initiation ceremony gone awry. At the risk of sounding impolite, please leave now."

Woojin quickly moved to join Bork in the lift-tube capsule, and the two acquaintances looked at each other sheepishly.

"Mac's Bones," Bork told the capsule, and then asked, "What was yours?"

"New recruit. Collapsed before the training even began. Do I gather that the tentacle chopper wasn't your first audition accident of the day?"

"Not even the first tentacle. If some of these youngsters had to fight in a real war—but no matter. It's a good thing I bumped into you. I meant to stop by the embassy to see your wife this evening, but our open tryouts turned into a bloodbath."

"We're on morning time, actually, so Lynx will be there another seven hours or so if you still have the energy. Anything I should know about?"

"I'm just a little uncertain about your seniority system now that the ambassador is away," the Drazen admitted. The capsule door slid open and he accompanied Woojin into the corridor that led to Mac's Bones. "I understand that Lynx is occupying Kelly's office and handling general inquiries, and I believe my report on EarthCent Intelligence suggests that your wife is a step closer to the, er, reins of power than you are."

"Lynx outranks me in everything," Woojin replied easily. "But she's helping out with the diplomatic branch this month, so if it's an intelligence issue and you couldn't get a hold of Clive or Blythe, I guess it's Thomas and then me."

"I'm sure Thomas won't mind if I ask you to pass this on, since I need to hurry back to the skirmish before somebody really gets hurt. We've been hearing disturbing rumors out of the Empire of a Hundred Worlds for some time that the tunnel network secessionists are planning some sort of action."

"Fleet versus the Imperials?"

"No, this relates to a long-standing schism about the Vergallian place amongst humanoid species. Our intelligence people will certainly be in touch with you about it in the near future, but given the large number of human mercenaries employed on Vergallian tech-ban worlds, not to mention your intelligence agents and Galactic Free Press reporters, I wanted to give you as much advance notice as possible. It's the sort of information I'd usually pass directly to Kelly, so as not to ruffle any feathers in the special relationship between our spy services."

"Thank you, Bork. I'll pass it on to Thomas and my wife, and I'll ping Clive and Blythe, though they're officially on vacation. I think they've been organizing their lives around their daughter's dance practices for the last few years, but with Samuel gone for the month, their schedule has opened up."

"Tough business, competitive dancing," Bork acknowledged. "I only wish some of the would-be warriors I saw today had better footwork. Speaking of which, I have to run."

The Drazen returned to the lift tube, and Woojin headed into Mac's Bones to reassure the trainees that their fellow was on his way to a full recovery.

# Three

Kelly's mother picked up the McAllisters at the space-port in a floating sedan with three rows of seats. The vehicle drew envious looks from everybody waiting at the platform.

"Is this your floater or a rental, Marge?" Joe asked as soon as they were underway.

"Mine. Didn't I tell you? The company gave it to me for free in return for making a commercial."

"You were in a commercial, Mom?" Kelly asked.

"I keep a copy in the onboard entertainment system," Marge replied, and then spoke directly at the dashboard. "Floater. Play my commercial."

A display panel slid up out of the chassis, blocking their forward vision. Kelly grabbed the dashboard and shrieked, causing her mother to look over in concern. "Floater. Pause commercial. Kelly. What's wrong?"

"You can't see where you're driving!"

"I'm not driving, dear. My reaction time is hardly good enough to run a floater at several hundred miles an hour, and that's if I could even see far enough ahead to make a difference. This sedan is equipped with full autopilot. Didn't you hear me say, 'Floater. Let's go,' when you got in?"

"I thought you were just telling us that it was a floater, in case we didn't know or something."

"Really, Kelly. Sometimes I think you just aren't paying attention. Floater. Resume commercial."

The screen lit up with a scene of a luxury floater, apparently the exact model in which they were riding, zipping along above the broken roads of a rough-looking section of urban sprawl. A monster loomed out of the wreckage of a large building and made a grab at the speeding conveyance, but the floater causally went through a series of smooth evasive maneuvers, dodging the tentacles and claws. The camera zoomed in on Marge, who was sitting sideways on the front bench seat, reading a book. She looked up and smiled.

"Hi, I'm Marge Frank, Ambassador Kelly McAllister's mom. When I take a trip, I always travel in my Chiangan Floater. It's based on Dollnick engineering and assembled by humans right here on Earth. I was so impressed that I bought ten shares in the company. Best of all, a small portion of the proceeds from every sale go to support the EarthCent diplomatic service. Take it from the mother of an ambassador. If Prince Drume approves, it's got to be good."

The cameras zoomed back out as the floater crossed a river, flying along next to a decrepit suspension bridge with dangling cables and gaps in the roadbed. As the floater passed, debris fell from the bridge, and an old car occupied by screaming passengers plunged into the river. The airbags inflated when it hit the water.

"You told everybody that I endorse Chiangan Floaters?" Kelly asked in dismay. "How could you?"

"I told everybody that Prince Drume endorses Chiangan Floaters. I know it for a fact because that nice Chiangan mayor who came to Earth to set up the factory, Bob was his name, arranged for me to meet the prince when I visited to pick out the color scheme for the uphol-stery. Do you like it?"

"I like it, Grandma," Samuel offered from the third row of seats which he had taken over for himself. "Can we watch the commercial again?"

"No, we cannot watch the commercial again," Kelly said. "Floater. Lower the screen. Floater!" She thumped the dashboard in frustration. "It doesn't listen to me."

"Floater. Imprint Kelly McAllister. Say something, Kelly."

"I'm not happy about this," Kelly grumbled.

"Operator Kelly McAllister registered," the floater an-nounced in a female voice that sounded suspiciously like Libby when she was answering the pings for InstaSitter.

"Floater. Imprint Joe McAllister," Marge continued.

"Hi, Floater," Joe said.

"Operator Joe McAllister registered."

"Floater. Lower screen," Kelly instructed.

The screen slid back down into the chassis, and the am-bassador saw that they had left the spaceport behind and were streaking north above a broad swath of asphalt that had seen better years.

"How about me?" Samuel demanded.

"I'm sorry, Sam, but you have to be sixteen to operate a floater on Earth. How old are you now?"

"Sixteen," the boy replied.

"Fourteen," Kelly said with finality. "Have you en-dorsed any other products as my mother?"

"Just a few," Marge hedged. "You've become very fa-mous on Earth, you know. Reporters contact me almost every day looking for filler to spice up articles they're writing. Since the Galactic Free Press started licensing

25

content to the media here, you're in the news all of the time."

Kelly groaned and buried her head in her hands.

"Tired, Kel?" Joe asked. "It looks like the middle section of this seat folds down, so if you want to move back a row and stretch out, you can take a nap."

"It's automatic," Marge informed them happily. "Floater. Open center, front row."

The seatback behind Kelly began to recline gently, and the ambassador gave up arguing and let the vehicle do its thing. A minute later, she was able to pull her legs through and lay full-length on the plush middle bench seat.

"This is pretty nice," she admitted, closing her eyes. "No seatbelts?"

"At this speed, they wouldn't help," Marge said, winking at Joe. "Just kidding. The floater is loaded with safety systems. Do you want to watch the owner's manual?"

"No, I'll just take a short nap."

"Do you still like to listen to the ocean when you go to sleep?"

"I haven't done that since I married Joe."

"I never knew that about you," her husband said. "What other secrets has she been hiding from me, Marge?"

"First things first," Kelly's mother said. "Floater. Play ocean sounds, center row, full isolation."

"I don't think it worked," Joe said.

"Full isolation includes an acoustic suppression field, in this case just for the second row. Can you hear us, Samuel?"

"Yes, Grandma."

"Do you want to come up front?"

"No. I'm just going to play with my robot a bit before I take a nap." Samuel had packed his toy robot from the

Libbyland gift shop over his mother's objections, wrapping it in a sweater and making space by removing most of the clothes she had insisted he bring. "Can I have the acoustic suppression thing too?"

"Floater. Third row. Full isolation," Marge instructed. "You're not tired, Joe?"

"I slept half the time on the Vergallian freighter. So, are we headed for Lisa's?" Joe asked, naming Kelly's younger sister.

"No, I thought I'd take you out to see Steve's final resting place and get it out of the way. You know that Kelly would end up organizing her whole vacation around it otherwise. Is she still mad at me for not inviting her to her father's funeral?"

"No, she got over that months ago," Joe lied. "I explained to her that your husband wanted to be buried no later than sunset the day after he passed, so there was no way she could have gotten to Earth on time. Besides, I remember Steve telling me that after attending funerals for most of his friends and relatives, he had no patience left for any of that stuff, and he wanted to keep it as simple as possible."

"That's right. I don't want to sound morbid, but we had plenty of time to prepare, and we both agreed that we wanted our bodies to be returned to the earth, where nature could get some use out of them. That's why we sponsored a grove in one of the new Frunge forests up North."

"Something wrong with the local cemeteries?"

"They all bury people in concrete boxes!" Marge exclaimed, looking extremely irritated. "They still sell you a wooden coffin if you want one, but they put that inside of a concrete box that's supposed to protect the groundwater

27

or keep the lawn in the cemetery from sagging—I could never get a straight answer out of them. I think it's really just some law passed by concrete box makers."

"And the Frunge?"

"If you sponsor a new grove, you get internment rights for your extended family. They don't allow wood coffins, of course, you know the Frunge, but any natural winding sheet or bag is acceptable. Steve chose burlap, but I'm planning on linen myself. Burlap is so scratchy."

"How did you find out about it?"

"The Frunge advertised. There was a big uproar from the cemetery trade associations when the ads started, but it died down pretty quickly after it became apparent that most people actually want a wooden coffin or a cremation urn, not to mention the fact that the Frunge don't allow headstones. And sponsoring a grove isn't cheap"

"What did it cost?"

"Well," Marge said, glancing over the seat at her sleeping daughter. "We intended to pay, but they ended up giving us the grove for free in return for a promotional spot. And they didn't charge for the Frunge tree warden who dug the grave and helped lay my husband to rest. All of the family plans on being buried there now, and you're welcome to join us."

"I'd kind of like to see my kids grow up first, but I'll keep it in mind. Kelly still talks about being ejected into space in her LoveU chair, though I don't take her seriously." He turned and looked over the seats. "I guess Sam is lying down since I can't see him."

"Floater. View back seat," Marge commanded.

The screen slid up out of the chassis again, and Joe would have sworn it showed his teenage son crouched on the floor behind the second row of seats before the image twitched and displayed Samuel stretched out on his stomach, fast asleep.

"Can we get the news on this thing?" Joe asked. "I really don't keep up with what's going on here, outside of what gets reported in the Galactic Free Press."

"Floater. Play the children's news."

"Floater. Pause," Joe interrupted. "Children's news?"

"The Children's News Network," Marge explained. "It's the only news I can stand watching these days. The other networks are all full of smiling people trying to top each other at who can report the most terrible story. I hate to say it, but the news became unwatchable after EarthCent convinced the Grenouthians to open an immersive technology center in New York."

"I know the bunnies go in for sensationalistic coverage, but it's hard to believe that they're worse than humans."

"It's not so much the current news as the archival footage," Marge explained. "The Grenouthians have been recording every war and disaster around the galaxy for millions of years, and the human networks seem determined to run each and every tragedy. The anchors rush through a minute or two of news, and then it's all highlights from the history of galactic misfortunes. They don't even bother pretending to draw connections to current events anymore."

Joe nodded. "I can see that happening. Floater. Continue."

A teenage girl with a serious expression and brown ponytails sitting alone at a news desk appeared on the screen. She looked directly at the camera, apparently reading from a teleprompter.

"...and the building has been condemned for multiple safety violations. Students are being reassigned to other local schools, and applications to the new Verlock magnet academy in the greater Cleveland region have spiked up over a thousand percent. Now to our special correspondent at EarthCent Headquarters, who will be reporting on the first Conference of EarthCent Ambassadors next week. Leon?"

A tall boy who was perhaps sixteen appeared on the screen, the image slightly off center, as if he had set up a camera himself and moved around to stand in front of it. Behind him was a wall plaque reading, "EarthCent Headquarters," with an arrow pointing to the right, and "QuickU Personality Enhancements," with an arrow pointing to the left.

"Thank you, Deborah," Leon responded. "I'm here in front of EarthCent headquarters in the city that never sleeps, but apparently our diplomatic service doesn't know that because the door is locked. Wait, I think the president is approaching right now. Sir?"

A sheepish-looking President Beyer holding a large take-out coffee moved into the picture. He rubbed his cheek to test the state of his beard stubble, since his habit was to shave at his desk with a Drazen device which he had been given as a gift by a visiting businessman. The current thinking at EarthCent headquarters was that gifts from aliens weren't considered bribes as long as they didn't leave the building.

"Leon, is it?" the president asked.

If the teenager was impressed that the president remembered his name from their single previous encounter at a ribbon-cutting ceremony, he didn't show it.

"President Beyer. Next Monday marks the official opening of your Conference of EarthCent Ambassadors. This will be the first real chance for most of us to see humanity's government, or the closest thing we have to a government out there, in action. Can you give us a preview of the events?"

"Well, it's not a constitutional convention, you know," the president said, trying to lower the audience's expectations. "I think we have some pretty interesting sessions planned." He stole a sip from his coffee before observing. "You're here pretty early. If you had made an appointment with Hildy, you wouldn't have been stuck waiting in the hall."

"Hildy Greuen," Leon spoke directly into the camera. "EarthCent's Director of Public Relations and your mistress."

"Er, yes," the president replied. "Would you like to come in and set up, and perhaps we could start over?"

"It's a live broadcast," the boy informed him. "Back to you, Deborah."

"Thank you, Leon. We'll have a full interview with the president as soon as it's available. Now to the weather, as reported by YOU."

The scene cut to a little boy who was wearing a yellow slicker with a hood and jumping in a puddle. "It's raining in Boston," he yelled.

The image was quickly replaced by a teenage girl with a surfboard running towards the ocean. "Sunny in Malibu," she informed them.

Then came a whole group of children, bundled up warmly, putting the finishing touches on a snowman. "It's cold in Denver," they shouted in rough unison, and then dissolved into laughter.

A boy with a homemade fishing rod, sitting on the end of a dock, reported. "Hot in Mississippi. And humid."

31

"We'll be back with more news after this brief message from our sponsor," Deborah announced.

"Aren't they cute?" Marge prompted her son-in-law.

"I liked the kid jumping in the puddle," Joe admitted.

An impossibly beautiful woman in a diaphanous dress appeared on the screen and halted mid-twirl, as if she had been surprised by the intrusion of a camera into her dance routine.

"Boys," she said. "Wouldn't you like to be popular with the girls and learn the confidence that will let you become great men? Girls. Wouldn't it be nice to meet some boys who won't step on your toes and ruin your shoes? Astria's Academy of Dance is now accepting applications for a local branch near you. Learn the techniques that have won the galactic ballroom prize every year since, well, longer than your planet has had written language. If you don't have the means to pay, Astria's academy is a member of the human barter network and a proud sponsor of the Children's News Network."

"Floater. Pause," Marge instructed the machine. "That reminds me. My husband said some funny things towards the end, so I couldn't always tell whether he was making things up or just confusing his memories. He would look at me and say, 'Marge. My grandson and I have a secret, and I'm not telling.' Then he would do that zipper thing across his lips and not speak to me until the next time he wanted something."

"And you think it has to do with dancing? Samuel still takes lessons with Blythe's daughter, you know. They compete on a regular schedule, though both of them insist they'll never be able to beat the top Vergallian juniors because they started too late."

"Steve left your son a special bequest," Marge said. "It's an antique cane that he picked up at an estate sale and walked with when he felt unsteady. He said Samuel could use it to impress his little girlfriend. I suspect he confused ballroom dancing with the tap routines from old movies where Fred Astaire would dance with a top hat and a cane, but it was one of his last wishes."

"I'm sure Sam will appreciate the gift, even if he can't use it for dancing. I know he really enjoyed the time he got to spend with his grandfather when you both came to visit."

Joe spent the next hour answering his mother-in-law's questions about Dorothy and their friends on Union Station. Eventually, the floater interrupted with the message, "Arriving at the Frank Grove in one minute."

"We better wake them up," Marge said. "Floater. Cancel acoustic suppression fields." The sound of gentle ocean waves filled the passenger compartment. "Floater. Cancel ocean."

The change in audio input was enough to wake Kelly, who sat up groggily and asked, "Are we here already?"

"Just another minute, dear," her mother replied. "Are you up back there, Samuel?"

Samuel's head popped up over the seat and he looked around. "Where are we?"

"We're almost at the Frank Grove, where your grandfather is buried," Marge replied.

"Good. I can visit him," the boy said.

"I thought we were going to Lisa's house," Kelly protested, rubbing the sleep from her eyes.

"We are, just as soon as we're finished here."

The floater slowed to a halt, and the Dollnick force field powered down, allowing the scent of fresh forest air to fill the vehicle. The occupants stepped out over the low gunwales onto the soft forest floor. Kelly wondered at how the floater had ended up in the midst of so many trees, and then she stepped to the side and saw the trunks all aligned in rows until the perspective was lost in the distance.

"The trees are all planted on a grid," Kelly objected.

"The Frunge tree warden told me that there's no point in trying to make a new forest look natural when it's not. But in a thousand years, nobody will know that this area was once deforested by surface mining," Marge replied.

"Frunge?" Kelly asked.

"Your mother explained to me that your family has purchased a burial grove here and we're welcome to use it," Joe fibbed. "I think it's a beautiful spot."

"Where's Grandpa?" Samuel asked.

"A little to your right and down a bit," Marge replied. "He's in front of the sign."

"This grove was made possible by a generous donation from the Frank family," Kelly read out loud. "Well, if that's what he wanted for a memorial…"

"It's what they allow. But the tree warden insisted on performing a Frunge ritual after your father was buried. He even brought a giant wooden pole and tossed it so that it bounced once and then fell across the grave."

"We can't even make a little border of stones or something?"

"Your father didn't want that and neither do I," Marge said. She took a small silver flask out of her purse and poured a liquid that smelled suspiciously like single malt Scotch onto the earth. "Don't ask. Come on, Samuel. Help an old woman take a little walk and let your Mom spend some time with her father before we head back. Coming, Joe?"

# Four

"Good morning, David," Aisha said, looking up from the stove where she was preparing breakfast. "You're here early today. I'm not even sure if Dorothy is up yet. But where are your shoes?"

"Uh," David stuttered, looking suddenly embarrassed.

"Hey, you're blocking the doorway," Paul said, moving around the young man and going over to see what Aisha was cooking.

"I want yogurt," Fenna announced, skipping into the kitchen and positioning herself in front of one of the high stools. She turned and looked at David, and then commanded, "Up."

Dorothy's boyfriend obligingly lifted the girl onto the stool, acutely conscious that Aisha's eyes had never left him.

"Did you stay over?" Aisha asked suspiciously.

"Uh," David replied, shuffling his bare feet and looking to Paul for help.

"Dorothy is twenty-one and they've been dating for nearly five years," Paul reminded his wife, throwing in a little shoulder rub to ease her obvious tension. "You were only nineteen when we got married."

"Married," Aisha repeated. "Is it a coincidence, David, that I'm seeing you here in the morning for the first time when Dorothy's parents are away?"

35

"That's not..." David muttered, backing towards the door.

"Sit," Paul instructed, and then gave his wife a kiss on the cheek. "You're cute when you get all traditional," he informed her.

Aisha's nut-brown complexion darkened noticeably. "And what did Beowulf have to say about all of this?"

"He's on a sleepover," Dorothy answered, crowding into the kitchen and going over to lean against David. After registering the look of disapproval on Aisha's face, the girl added by way of explanation, "Brinda invited Beowulf to keep company with their Cayl hound."

"It looks like you're making more than enough roti for everybody," Paul said, pointing to the growing mound of flat breads that his wife had continued to prepare, even as she carried out the interrogation.

"I invited the Cohans for breakfast to talk about their son and his little Stryx friend appearing on my show."

"That's a great idea," Dorothy said. "I'll go set the table. Come on, David."

"Mikey is coming?" Fenna asked.

"They'll be here in around five minutes," Aisha confirmed. "Do you want to go greet them since Beowulf is away?"

"Okay." The girl carefully climbed down from the high stool, holding onto the counter with one hand, and then ran out of the kitchen.

The moment Fenna exited the room, Aisha asked, "Do you really think it's okay for David to stay over with her parents away?"

"Sure, I'm surprised he hasn't before. I guess he's still scared of Joe."

"Or Beowulf. Well, I suppose David can eat the dog's share this morning. Will you start putting out the side dishes?"

A few minutes later, Fenna ran up the ice harvester's ramp with Mike and Spinner in hot pursuit. Shaina and Daniel followed with the baby at a more sedate pace, and everybody sat down to a home-cooked Indian breakfast.

"It feels so weird being here without Kelly," Shaina commented. "I still remember the first time she came to the Shuk shopping for counterfeits and my Dad asked me to take her around."

"I'm just hoping that Joe talked to you about the poker game," Daniel said, looking over at Paul. "I think I'm finally getting a feel for Dring's tells. Toughest alien I ever played against."

"I promised Dad I'd put out the tables and handle refreshments, but Stanley is going to take his seat," Paul replied. "How are the preparations going for your conference this year?"

For the next ten minutes, the EarthCent consul monopolized the conversation with a detailed report on the evolution of the Sovereign Human Communities Conference, pausing only long enough to inhale a mouthful of food at occasional intervals. Shaina shrugged apologetically at the others, but everyone knew how important the conference had become to Daniel, and they enjoyed his enthusiasm. He wrapped up his report with a funny story about how the humans living on an open Dollnick world had taken to using alien idioms, such as "two arms short" for a half-baked business plan, and then headed off to the embassy in a rush, because he had a holo-conference scheduled.

Fenna, Mike, and Spinner all disappeared under the table to play a secret game, and David excused himself to leave for work. Dorothy and Shaina got into a discussion about shoe development for SBJ Fashions, and Jeeves floated in just as Aisha was working up her nerve to make a pitch to the little Stryx.

"Morning, Jeeves," Paul said. "Are you going to help me with repairs today? We're not taking in any new ships while Joe is gone, and I'd like to clean this lot out before the weekend."

"I thought perhaps you could use an extra hand, or at least a pincer," Jeeves responded. "I hope I'm not interrupting anything."

"Did you know I was planning on asking Spinner to appear on my show?" Aisha inquired.

"Libby might have mentioned something. As long as I'm already here, I'd be honored to assist if I could."

"Does that mean you think it's a good idea?"

"I think all of your ideas are good ideas," Jeeves replied, laying it on thick.

"I'm going out to make the morning rounds," Paul announced, figuring that if he wasn't in the room, there would be less chance of being blamed for anything Jeeves did or didn't do. "Let me know if you need anything."

Aisha examined Jeeves closely, and for a moment, she considered asking him to leave. Then the children emerged from their table-cave, and she decided to just proceed as planned.

"Mike, Spinner. Could you guys come over here for a minute?"

The boy and the little Stryx came and stood before Aisha, their body language suggesting that they had been caught red-handed in some crime. Spinner lived up to his name by rotating nervously in one direction and then the other as he floated in place, and Aisha had to suppress the urge to ask what they had been doing under the table.

"Spinner," she began. "Did you know that Mike is going to start appearing on 'Let's Make Friends' with our next cast change?"

The little Stryx bobbed and ventured a creaky, "Yes, Mrs. McAllister."

"Aisha," she corrected him gently. "Did you know that we've never had a little Stryx on the show?"

Spinner stopped spinning and began to vibrate alarmingly. "You haven't?"

"I was thinking that if you're interested, you could come on the cast with Mike."

"I could?"

"It would be fun. We play games and tell stories. I'm sure you've seen the show."

"Yes," the little Stryx replied, sinking to the floor.

"Are you alright?" Aisha asked in alarm.

"Nobody floats on your show," Spinner said, and began tipping from one side to the other like a wobbly toy figure.

"That's because they don't know how," Aisha explained. "We don't have a rule against floating. Of course, you would be welcome to move any way you like."

Spinner popped back up into the air and immediately started doing three-quarter turns to the left and right. "Teacher says it's okay," he rasped.

"Do you mean Libby? I discussed it with her before asking." Aisha relaxed a little, and continued with the question she asked all new cast members. "What do you like to do?"

"Go to school, and play with Mikey and Fenna."

"Anything else?"

"Was that the wrong answer?" the little Stryx chirped nervously. "I've never been asked to be on a show before. I don't know what I'm doing."

"There is no right or wrong response. I just want to get an idea of what you like to do."

"How can there be no right or wrong?" Spinner's constant motion came to a dead stop. "Did I just fail?"

"You're doing fine," Aisha reassured the little Stryx, but she glanced over at Jeeves for support.

"Think of it this way," Jeeves suggested, seizing the chance to jump into the conversation. "Say you were in a boat with two humans and they both fell in. Which one would you save?"

"Jeeves!" Aisha said angrily.

"Fell in where?" Spinner asked.

"Wherever the boat was," Jeeves replied. "Humans are always falling out of boats."

"Is one of them Mikey?" the little Stryx wanted to know. The boy stopped teasing Fenna and stood a little straighter at the mention of his name.

"Maybe they're both Mike."

"So it's a multi-dimensional math problem," Spinner declared in relief. "Can I have time to work it out?"

"Never mind the boat," Aisha said. "I just want to make sure that you're comfortable using your imagination since we do a lot of that on the show."

"You want me to lie? Libby teaches us to tell the truth whenever practical."

"Imagination isn't lying," Dorothy interjected. "Shaina and I were talking about creating new shoes just now, so we have to use our imaginations."

Spinner swung about in the direction of the fashion designer and the businesswoman and inspected their feet. "But your shoes don't look broken," he objected.

"Oh, I have lots of shoes. And we aren't creating them just for us, but for everybody who likes new shoes. We want to produce a unique product that doesn't already exist."

The little Stryx paused to absorb this latest nugget of information. "You want to make new shoes that aren't really shoes?"

"Well, they'll still be shoes," Dorothy explained awkwardly. "We aren't designing new ones just for the sake of being different. They still have to fit our feet and make us look and feel good."

"And they have to sell," Jeeves reminded her.

"They're going to be better than the old shoes," Dorothy concluded energetically.

"Better how?"

"This is just like visiting Libby's school on Parents Day," Shaina commented with a laugh. "Spinner. I think you'll enjoy being on the show, and you can practice your imagination with Mike and Fenna before it starts so you don't make mistakes."

"I'll try it," the little Stryx rasped, resuming his pattern of partial spins. "Can I go practice making things up now?"

"I think that would be a good idea," Aisha replied, wondering if Spinner was going to put her through the third degree every time she asked a question on the show. She decided on the spot to develop a strategy for avoiding circular conversations, and made a mental note to warn the Grenouthian studio engineers about reflections coming off the young Stryx's constantly moving metal body.

41

"I'm still curious to know which Mike he's going to save from drowning," Jeeves said, looking after the children as they fled from the ice harvester to get away from the grownups.

"I should have known what a big help you were going to be," Aisha retorted, glaring at the Stryx. "Does his voice have to be that scratchy? Can you adjust it?"

"It's his voice, not a translation device," Jeeves replied. "Stryx don't communicate with one another through spoken words unless we're being polite to biologicals who happen to be present. Back when Libby started her experimental school for humans and used me as the guinea pig for the first Stryx student, she decided to let me develop my own audible voice, rather than simply mapping our communications onto English."

"But surely even the youngest Stryx has a larger vocabulary then pretty much anybody."

"It's not a vocabulary issue, it's about learning to communicate. Spinner's lack of vocal control just reflects the uncertainty he feels about what he's saying. Language conveys much more than simple facts, and it took me months just to understand how much of my feelings I should reveal in my voice. You should ask Libby to play back my introductory speech to the class. I sounded like a metallic rat being fed into a meat grinder."

"I remember a little from when I helped teach Metoo to speak," Dorothy volunteered. "I was only four, and I didn't understand that Metoo was really better than me at everything except for socializing with humans. It's the one built-in skill we have that Stryx don't."

"That's why Libby has been slowly raising the age of the school children she pairs with the young Stryx," Jeeves explained. "Your brother was five when he got Banger as

42

his work/play assignment, and Mike was nearly six when he started with Spinner. It's really cut down on the number of little Stryx getting emotionally overloaded and shutting themselves off, which saves me a lot of running around to wake them."

"Is there any chance that Spinner will shut himself off on my show?" Aisha asked. "I wouldn't want to traumatize hundreds of billions of children."

"There's always a chance, but Spinner strikes me as quite stable, if you'll pardon the pun."

"What pun?"

"He means gyroscopically," Shaina explained. "After working with Jeeves for ten years, I've gotten used to his humor. You can take Stryx out of the physics, but you can't take the physics out of the Stryx."

"But what if something happened and he did shut himself off?" Aisha asked. "I've had cast members fall asleep on set, but the other children wake them up. It's almost a rite of passage with young Fillinducks because the lighting makes them drowsy."

"I could come to the studio while you're shooting, just to be on hand," Jeeves offered.

Dorothy and Shaina both made faces and shook their heads at Aisha, but the host of 'Let's Make Friends,' either didn't see, or she was so worried about Spinner becoming catatonic on her show that she didn't care.

"Thank you, Jeeves. That's a relief. But if he really has access to all of the Stryx knowledge and doesn't always understand what he's saying, what if he lets out some technical secret on the show? It's a live broadcast, and I wouldn't want to be responsible for everybody learning how to create black holes at home using common kitchen cleaners."

"You'd need gazillions of tons of kitchen cleaners to create a black hole," Jeeves replied, sketching a circle in the air with his pincer, as if to mentally encompass the project. "And there aren't any two-word answers to the secrets of the multiverse."

"But what if, say, the Stryx know that the disappearance of that Horten colony ship a few cycles back was actually due to an alien attack, and not a technical failure," Aisha persisted, trying to come up with a worst case scenario. "If a little Horten asked a question about it on the show and Spinner answered truthfully, it could start a war!"

"There's always a transmission delay," Jeeves replied, and then clicked his pincer a few times. "Oops, Libby says the delay was a secret, so don't tell the Grenouthians."

"But I thought the show was broadcast in real-time over the Stryxnet," Aisha protested. "It's instantaneous."

"Paul and his friends couldn't have played Raider/Trader using ship controllers if there was a lag," Dorothy pointed out.

"It's not a technical limitation. It's an introduced delay, just for network broadcasts. I believe that on Earth they used to call it a 'tape delay,' and it gave the censors time to bleep bad language."

"You're censoring my show?"

"Not your show, everybody's shows," Jeeves reassured her, and then continued to talk out loud, even though it was obvious he was addressing one of the older Stryx. "Alright, I shouldn't have said anything, but now that they know, the least I can do is to clarify the situation. What do you mean this should be a private conversation? Oh, sorry. I do it now without even noticing. Yes, seriously. No, I do not have my pincer manipulators crossed. I do? Well, I'm still right."

"Are you really talking to somebody, or are you practicing a stand-up act?" Dorothy asked suspiciously.

"Do you think I have potential?" Receiving no reply, Jeeves let out an exaggeratedly mechanical sigh and continued. "There's no delay on game data or direct communications since they utilize point-to-point addressing. Our concern is strictly with broadcasts. Not long after the first-generation Stryx began selling real-time communications bandwidth, one of the probationary species on the original version of our tunnel network used a popular sitcom to broadcast instructions to their expatriates to instantly launch attacks against various host species. You're talking tens of millions of years before my time, but it was quite an embarrassment."

"The Grenouthians assured me that they pay top cred for real-time," Aisha insisted.

"It is real-time," Jeeves replied. "Just with a delay."

"I'll bet your elders think you're the one who needs a tape delay," Shaina commented.

"Don't give them any ideas," the Stryx replied, sounding suddenly nervous. "You know that Libby is a terrible eavesdropper."

"So you're saying that Spinner probably won't put himself into a coma, and that if he blurts out anything that he shouldn't, Libby or Gryph will just censor it," Aisha summarized. "But what could they use to fill in the gap?"

"Public service announcements," Jeeves said, and lowered his speech register to that of a professional announcer. "This is a reminder to keep your personal belongings with you at all times while transiting stations on the tunnel network. Help keep space clean and give our lost-and-found employees a break."

Dorothy giggled and slapped the Stryx on his casing. "Stop it."

"But what about the people and the aliens on the station and in the studio audience?" Aisha pressed on. "I know that not everybody in the six-to-eight age demographic watches, but we still win the station ratings every cycle."

"Gryph would just flood the station with forget-it gas and swear the unaffected AI to secrecy," Jeeves replied. "It's easy to wipe the last few minutes from the memories of biologicals. There's a Farling physician with a shop on the arrivals concourse who sells all that stuff cheap."

"Are you serious?" Shaina asked.

"It appears I really have said too much," Jeeves replied. "Sorry to have to do this."

There was a sharp popping sound, and a tube shot out of the Stryx's casing and sprayed a cloud of bright white gas at the women. It smelled like almonds, and it made them all sneeze exactly five times.

"What was that stuff?" Dorothy demanded as soon as the sneezing subsided.

"See? You've forgotten already."

"I haven't forgotten anything," she said irritably. "You tape delay broadcasts and..." Dorothy trailed off as she saw Jeeves flickering his casing lights in silent electronic laughter. "Alright, you got me that time."

# Five

"Do you have any plans yet for today?" Marge asked her daughter. "I thought you might want to visit the Drazen factory complex in Rochester. They've completely rebuilt the old industrial area."

"That dip Bork brought to the last poker game was a Drazen Foods export from Earth," Joe reminded his wife. "The ambassador said that his friend Glunk was raking it in by the tentacle load, which I'm guessing is a good thing. I'll bet he gives us the grand tour."

"He offered through Bork before we left the station, so we have an open invitation for any time this week," Kelly replied. "Are you sure you're up to it, Mom? There will probably be plenty of walking."

"Walking is how I keep on living, Kelly. But I've already been on that tour several times because it's on the circuit for our investor's club. I'm supposed to be the expert on alien venture capital opportunities, though why anybody is willing to take advice from an eighty-year-old woman is beyond me."

Kelly tried to reconcile her mother's stated age with her birth date and concluded that one of them was off by nearly ten years, but she wisely let it pass. Instead she asked, "How will we get there?"

"You'll take my floater, of course. I'm sorry that the commercial wasn't to your liking, but I hope you don't hold that against the product. It really is the only way to travel."

"Thanks, Marge," Joe answered for Kelly. "I'd like to visit that factory, and I want Samuel to have a chance to see some of the countryside before we head into the city for the EarthCent conference."

"I won't expect you back until supper, then. Have a good time."

Ten minutes later, after confirming the invitation with Glunk's human secretary, Kelly gave the floater its marching orders. The craft smoothly navigated its way through the light traffic in her mother's neighborhood until it reached an interstate onramp. There it elevated above the warning barrier and began rocketing along the broken old highway towards Rochester, staying just high enough to get over the heaves and occasional jagged pieces sticking up from the surface of the road without having to continually adjust its altitude.

"Your mother has a fine eye for transportation," Joe pronounced after a few minutes of silky smooth travel. "Any idea where the factory for these things is located? I wouldn't mind visiting."

"Mom mentioned that it's on the west coast," Kelly replied. "I think the Dollnicks took over some huge complex that manufactured military airplanes back before the Stryx opened Earth, though I guess there wasn't much left standing by this time."

"Can't be more than an hour away by sub-orbital," Joe replied. "The artificial Sharf guy who sells me new engine parts said that they moved a mothballed factory to Earth to manufacture sub-orbital craft. It sounds like the president's strategy of welcoming an alien invasion is really paying

48

off, since he's drawing species that aren't even members of the tunnel network."

"Why are there so many burned-down houses?" Samuel asked from the middle seat, where he was staring out through the force field that served as a canopy while the floater was in motion.

"They were built of flammable materials, and when you take away the people, if one catches fire, it can burn down a whole neighborhood," his father explained. "Your grandfather told me that there had been problems with a lack of jobs up here long before the Stryx came. The whole area bordering the Great Lakes used to be the nation's manufacturing heartland, but at some point people started calling it the Rust Belt, due to all of the abandoned industrial sites."

"Because everybody left Earth?"

"Even before that, they moved south and west for warmer weather and different types of jobs," Joe said. "A lot of these cities were half-empty before people had the opportunity to leave Earth, and then they were among the hardest hit by emigration. Some pretty large areas have returned to nature, and the Frunge have been buying northern real estate to plant forests all around the globe."

"But why would the aliens open factories here if everything rusts or burns?" Samuel persisted.

"It's not the place, it's the economy," Kelly explained. "Didn't Libby teach you about this stuff in school?"

"I think we get to it this year. She said that the history of human economics gives younger kids nightmares."

"Well, the important thing to remember is that the same people who manufactured all sorts of things in this region a hundred years ago are now working in local factories for the Drazens and the Frunge."

49

"I didn't think people could live that long," Samuel said. "Are they using alien medical technology to stay alive, like we saw in Libbyland?"

"What?" Kelly reran the conversation in her head and identified the problem. "I didn't mean that the same individuals who were employed in manufacturing a century ago were still working today. I meant their grand-children and great-grandchildren."

"Oh. So why did their grandparents and great-grandparents lose their jobs?"

"Ask your father."

"Dad?"

"It mainly had to do with money, I think. Rather than investing in new factories and creating better products, some businesses moved to where they could find cheaper labor, and eventually, they sent most of the jobs overseas to poorer countries in search of short-term profits. Once manufacturing was the main contributor to the economy, but by the time the Stryx opened Earth, Stanley says that the financial industry dwarfed everything else."

"And what did they make?" Samuel asked.

"The financial industry? They made money, for them-selves mainly. I don't really understand it myself."

"I guess I'll ask Dorothy when we get back since she must have learned it already," the boy said, and resumed watching the landscape flash by. Joe and Kelly continued talking about the past, exchanging memories of half-forgotten stories from their childhoods, but they carefully avoided the subject of economics.

"Arriving at Drazen Foods in one minute," the floater announced, and shot up an old exit ramp littered with abandoned cars.

"This can't be it," Kelly said, gazing at the complex of gleaming white buildings and towers they were approaching. "It's too beautiful for a factory, and it's big enough to be a city."

"You know the Drazens like to do things right," Joe replied. "I wish this thing would go slower in parking lots, though."

The floater must not have been programmed to respond to wishes, because it sped down the center aisle without hesitation, and then pulled up under a canopy. A young man wearing blue coveralls waved as the vehicle came to a halt, and then stepped forward to identify himself.

"Hi. I'm Billy Ogden, Glunk's secretary. We spoke earlier this morning."

"Kelly McAllister," the ambassador introduced herself, stepping out of the floater. "My husband, Joe, and our son, Samuel. Is the floater alright here?"

"I take it you've never been in a modern parking lot," Billy said. "We're equipped with a Dollnick-compatible lot controller, assembled on Earth by human technicians. When you step away from the floater, the controller will park it."

"How will we find it again?" Samuel asked. "It's Grandma's floater, and she'll be mad if we lose it."

"The Dolly lot controller will bring it over as soon as you exit the building. No human walking or driving allowed in the parking lot, cuts the accident rate to zero. Shall we go in?"

Kelly and Joe followed the young man under the awning towards the factory entrance, but Samuel trailed behind, sneaking continual peeks over his shoulder to see where the floater ended up. Then he sprinted to catch his parents at the doors.

"So what products do you package here?" Joe asked the secretary. "I grew up in ranch country, and you're pretty far north and east of the main agricultural belts."

"There are advantages and disadvantages to all factory locations," Billy replied seriously. "Glunk was actually the first entrepreneur from any of the advanced species to get a factory up and running on Earth, and he told me that he wasn't entirely confident in the legal validity of the extraterritorial status the president granted. He decided to put the factory here mainly to stay in the same political entity as the EarthCent headquarters, in case there were problems."

"Pretty smart," Joe acknowledged.

"Plus, Glunk had, uh, reliable information that the Dollnicks were purchasing all of our inactive railroad rights of way, and with the upgrade to independently propelled floater boxcars, the whole continent got smaller in a hurry. We can get a load of chili peppers from New Mexico in less than twenty-four hours, or two days from Old Mexico."

"I don't remember an Old Mexico," Kelly said.

"It's a big place, south of New Mexico," the secretary replied seriously. "I think one of them may be a province of the other now, but I don't remember which. In any case, this whole complex is a standard prefab food processing plant that the Drazens include with every one of their colony ships. I was here from the first day, and the riggers had it up and running in less than three months. The parking lot took longer because the excavators hit ledge."

Billy continued walking forward rapidly as he talked and gestured. He managed to wave or nod to other humans and the occasional Drazen they passed, all dressed in blue jump suits. Suddenly, without any reason, Kelly began to cry.

"Hard to believe it was only three years ago that the president was pitching the idea to Glunk in our living room," Joe said, patting her on the back to comfort her.

Kelly looked at him through her tears and shook her head. "I'm not crying. Well, maybe I am crying, but it's not because of that."

"Hey, your face is really turning red," Billy said, suddenly concerned. "I can't believe I forgot about this." He reached in his pocket and whipped out a crumpled ball of plastic, which exploded into a pink blow-up doll the size of a person. He ran a finger down the back and it fell open, the limbs collapsing as it deflated. "Here, help me get her into the isolation suit," the secretary said to Joe.

"How will I breathe?" Kelly asked, as Billy worked her left leg into the suit while she balanced on her right with Joe's support.

"The whole transparent face section is a Horten microfilter that keeps out the airborne capsaicin molecules," Billy explained. "The filter also tends to trap the moisture from your breathing, so we'll get you out of it as soon as possible."

"Where are the peppers?" Samuel asked.

"They're actually in the next building," the secretary explained. "Your mother must be highly sensitive. This is the office building, and nobody has ever had a problem here before, at least that I can remember."

"It's probably from living on a space station for the last twenty-five years," Kelly said defensively. "I remember when I was a kid they said that children who grew up in super-clean environments were more prone to allergies."

"But you grew up a couple hundred miles from here," Joe pointed out. "And the Stryx don't over-scrub the air for just that reason." Kelly would have glared at him, but her eyes were watering too much.

"Just let me get your other arm in—and done," Billy said, pulling the hood over her head from the front to the back, and then running his thumb all the way down her spine to seal the suit. "How's that?"

"My eyes are still watering," Kelly complained, her voice unchanged by speaking through the Horten filter. She took a few experimental steps and found that the suit was so lightweight and flexible, that aside from the feeling that a feather was tickling the tip of her nose, she was barely aware that she had it on.

"It will take a minute or two before the molecules that already reached you get diluted. And here we are," the guide concluded, ushering them into an office.

The décor was pure Drazen, with a number of battleaxes and other primitive weapons affixed to the walls, but the suit of armor in the corner was obviously of human manufacture, since the gauntlets had five fingers and there was no opening for a tentacle. Glunk was engaged in a holo-conference as they entered, but he immediately excused himself and waved the projection out of existence.

"Ambassador McAllister and family. I am honored by your presence." The Drazen made a theatrical bow before stepping forward to shake hands with the guests. "My old friend Ambassador Bork contacted me weeks ago about your planned trip and I asked him to relay an invitation, but I wasn't sure you would actually find time to fit us in until this morning. I see that my secretary has erred on the side of caution by making you wear the environmental suit in the office building. I recalled your reaction to pepper

54

spray back on the station and wanted to make sure that you would be comfortable on the tour. But you seem to be a bit red."

"It's nothing," Kelly said, not wanting to get the secretary in trouble. "I can't believe how much you've accomplished here in three years. Bork is always bringing us new products from your factory."

"And Dad and I try to eat them," Samuel put in. "Mom thinks everything is too hot."

"Even our Turpoil?" Glunk asked in astonishment. "You can't keep Drazen children away from the stuff."

"Have we tried that one, Joe?" Kelly asked.

"It's their house brand of turpentine oil," Joe replied. "We give it to trainees to rub on sore muscles."

"Cassachips?" the Drazen inquired.

"Those are the dried slices of cassava root, right?" Kelly asked. "Bork loves those."

"Come on, boss," Billy said. "I keep telling you that cyanide is bad for humans. We can only eat cassava if it's prepared right, like for tapioca pudding."

"Black pearls?" Glunk suggested.

"Poisonous," the secretary replied, and added for the guests, "He means ackee seeds."

"We can't send them away empty handed after the tour," the Drazen cried in mock distress. "How about Fugusauce?"

"Now he's just showing off," Billy told the McAllisters. "It's made from the poisonous parts of pufferfish."

"There must be something I can tolerate." Kelly said. "Don't you have anything with chocolate?"

"We're running the fungus line today," the secretary ventured doubtfully. "Some of the mushrooms might be edible."

"Come, come," Glunk said, deciding that he had pushed his private joke about the inability of humans to eat their own produce far enough. "Let me show you the factory that you helped make possible. I'm sure I don't need to tell you that I've become a very wealthy Drazen thanks to this opportunity."

The McAllisters and the secretary followed Glunk out of his office and down the corridor to a door that looked like an airlock on an old spaceship. A large sign, in Drazen and English, read, "Decontamination." Billy pressed a prominent red button, and the outer door opened with a hiss.

"I didn't know Drazens cared so much about food purity," Kelly commented, thinking to score some points for humanity after being reminded of their weak stomachs. The outer door closed and the inner door immediately opened without any noticeable decontamination process. "Was that it? No sprays or blowing air?"

"It's only used in the other direction, to protect the office workers who might be sensitive to the food processing byproducts," Billy explained, leading the group onto a catwalk that extended over the factory floor. "The workers in the production areas are all tested for reactions and allergies, and they suit up when we run the really nasty stuff."

"You shouldn't refer to our products that way," Glunk scolded his secretary. "Take the next right."

Samuel trailed behind, ogling the enormous mounds of red and green peppers of every shape and size being unloaded from large floaters that seemed to move about without anybody controlling them. Workers armed with tools ranging from shovels and pitchforks to what looked like giant vacuum cleaner hoses were moving peppers in every direction, and gleaming machines as large as houses were spitting out bottles and buckets of product, all neatly labeled, onto conveyer belts.

"It seems a terrible waste to me that all of our human workers insist on suiting up when we run perfumes," Glunk said, indicating a production line to the left. "Your biosphere is such an untapped treasure house for scents that we have to restrain ourselves from flooding the market. Have you seen the ads for our latest, the black bottle with the white stripe?"

"Eau de skunk?" Joe guessed.

"A dog wearing clothes!" Samuel cried excitedly, pointing at something in the perfume area. The group came to a halt, and the McAllisters stared as they realized there were a number of dogs dressed in white full body suits moving about the factory floor.

"The jewel in the crown of our perfume operations," Glunk said proudly. "You can't beat a dog's nose, they're even better than ours. We've employed extensive testing to identify some of the smartest pups on Earth. It's well worth the investment in training, and," the Drazen lowered his voice to a whisper, "they work for food and affection. I was afraid they might unionize in protest over having to wear the shedding containment suits, but nobody appreciates dog hair in a two-hundred-cred vial of perfume."

"Uh, boss?" Billy said, tapping the Drazen's elbow to get his attention. A few yards in front of them on the catwalk sat an intelligent looking German Shepherd in a shedding containment suit, her head cocked to the left, listening intently.

"As I was saying," Glunk proclaimed loudly. "Training the dogs is expensive, and they're eating me out of house and home, but their sense of smell is almost as good as our own." Then he ushered the humans forward, skirting the dog, who gave the Drazen entrepreneur a calculating look as they passed. When they reached a second airlock door at the end of a long catwalk, he looked around carefully before saying, "I keep forgetting about their hearing. Sometimes I take my lunch outside, and the instant I tear anything open, every dog on the factory grounds shows up to ask for some."

"The native Drazen dogs don't hear well?" Joe asked.

"It's an adaptation to our singing, I think," Glunk replied. "Not every Drazen woman is choir material, but that doesn't stop them from practicing day and night."

The airlock door hissed open, the group entered, and this time the decontamination procedures kicked in. First, an electric field made all of their hair stand up on end, though the hood of Kelly's environmental suit muted the full effect in her case. Then air began blowing through the heavy steel screening of the floor, increasing in speed until Joe had to put a hand on Samuel's shoulder to keep the boy from being lifted off his feet. Billy leaned toward the two and shouted, "Hold your breaths," and a few seconds later, the air filled with a silvery powder, which vanished almost as quickly as it appeared. Then the blowers stopped, and the outer airlock slid open.

"Did you inhale any of that?" Joe asked his wife.

"The Horten microfilter wouldn't allow it through," Billy assured them.

"Welcome to my side business," Glunk said, ushering them out of the airlock. "This isn't part of the regular tour since Drazen Foods is prime contractor in name alone, but Bork asked my help in cutting through the red tape for our Museum of Science and Technology. It turned out that the museum director acted a bit hastily when she offered your president the restoration job for the 'Long Shot.' Some busybody dug through the museum's charter and discovered that donated spacecraft must remain in Drazen custody at all times."

"Is that what we're looking at?" Kelly asked, trying to make sense of the jumble of linear antennas entwined in copper cables. "That thing is the first successful Drazen jump ship?"

"Just one of the focal nodes," the Drazen informed her. "There are thirty-six in all, and they're bringing them down one at a time for rewinding. I'm not a physics type myself, so don't ask me how it works."

"Don't look at me," Joe said, when Kelly and Samuel turned in his direction. "I can replace parts on the modern ones when they go out of spec, but I'm the last guy who could explain to you how they work. We didn't have a lot of time for advanced physics in the mercenaries, and I don't know if there's a human alive who really understands the math."

"At least one man is coming close," Glunk said. "The whole project is run by a fellow named Hep, who is here on a five-year contract. Your people found him on a Verlock open world, Fyndal, where he headed the human division of the academy. I'm afraid he's off at some academic conference this week trying to explain to your native physicists why general relativity is just a special case in any of the advanced models."

"By 'any of,' are you implying that there's more than one?" Kelly asked.

"Even I know that, Mom," Samuel said impatiently. "Did you think that the Drazens and the Verlocks and the Frunge and the Hortens all use the same system of physics? As the Vergallians say, 'There's more than one way to skin a rebellious peasant,' and none of the biologicals have a clue how Stryx multiverse math works, except for maybe the Cayl."

"I just thought that they had different names for the same physical laws," his mother said.

"Nope," the boy replied, before asking Glunk, "Is it okay if I record some pictures through my implant? It would make a really cool show-and-tell for my school."

# Six

"In conclusion, uh, following multiple reports of trouble brewing between imperial factions in the Vergallian Empire, we, I mean, EarthCent Intelligence, will be meeting with our counterparts in Drazen Intelligence to discuss the situation, and, uh, there's some talk of putting together a broad working group of interested species to stay abreast of the situation."

Lynx exhaled with relief and made a swiping motion to clear her notes from the display desk. She couldn't help wondering if Kelly had really done all of her weekly reports extemporaneously. Even with the script, she suspected some "uhs" and "I means" had crept in, but she had never thought of herself as a public speaker.

"Daniel is waiting to see you," Libby announced.

"Thanks. Why doesn't he come in?"

"You locked the door."

"Oh, I forgot. Can you open it?"

"I could, but it's traditional to do it yourself," the Stryx librarian explained.

Lynx got up and went to the door, waving her hand to disengage the proximity lock. It slid open immediately, and Daniel almost ran into her entering Kelly's office.

"Get through the report okay this time?" he asked.

"Yes, thank you. Second time's the charm, and the fill-in-the-blanks template you made for me really helped. Are you done for the week?"

"I have holo-conferences scheduled pretty much every day now," Daniel told her. "You've visited a number of open worlds, so you know how the humans living on them tend to go native. If I skip a single holo-conference, they end up arguing over whether to conduct the meetings by the Prince's Debate Rules, Choir Order or Stone Law, just to name three."

"I'm guessing that's Dollnick, Drazen, or Verlock procedures. So what system do you favor?"

"I just make it up as I go along and claim it's from EarthCent diplomatic training. Anyway, did you open your envelope from Kelly yet?"

"I knew I forgot something. Now where did I put it? Does this desk even have drawers?"

"Check your purse," Libby hinted.

"Thanks." The cultural attaché fished in her purse and brought out an envelope with 'Lynx' printed on it. "I've been carrying this around since Kelly gave it to me almost two weeks ago, and I forgot about it. Were we supposed to open them right away?"

"I think so," Daniel replied. "Take a look at mine."

Lynx accepted the note and read, "If you and Donna can't figure something out and Libby won't help for noninterference reasons, ask Bork, Czeros, or Srythlan. If you're really desperate, try Jeeves. If you have extra time, Daniel is overloaded with conference work and can use a hand." She stopped and looked up. "Kelly gave you the wrong note?"

"What does your say?"

Lynx checked the envelope carefully and noted with relief that the flap hadn't been glued down. "I had a bad experience once with one of these things," she explained, fishing out the note and passing it to Daniel.

"Don't start any wars," he read. "Hah. Hah. Lynx will have her hands full doing two jobs when Clive and Blythe go on semi-vacation, so don't load her down with conference work. Remember that Donna has been here longer than any of us and knows more about how the system works than I do."

"She gives decent advice," Lynx commented grudgingly.

"What's a semi-vacation?" Daniel asked.

"Clive and Blythe took the twins camping in Libbyland, so they're only a ping away if we need to talk to them. But I'm supposed to be in charge of EarthCent Intelligence while they're on vacation, with Thomas as second in command."

"I thought Wooj was right behind Clive," Daniel said.

"Apparently, so did he," Lynx remarked dryly. "It's always been Clive, then Blythe, then me, then Thomas. Since we're primarily an information-gathering organization, all of the day-to-day work is handled by the analysts in the main office. Woojin sort of points them at strategic gaps we need to fill in, and he reads all of the reports, but Clive is the one who answers to the steering committee."

"Visitor," Libby announced. "It's Dring."

Lynx and Daniel exchanged looks, then went together to meet the Maker at the door. As the only local representative of the species that had created the Stryx, Dring was venerated by many of the aliens as a sort of demigod, and his shape-shifting nature only increased their awe. But living as he did in a corner of Mac's Bones, he had become a familiar figure to the humans who were friends with the ambassador's family.

"Good evening, Mrs. Cultural Attaché, Mr. Consul," Dring addressed them formally. "I hope I'm not interrupting anything."

"Please come in, Dring," Lynx said, trying not to betray the nervousness she felt about the Maker seeking her out at the embassy. "Is there something wrong?"

"The matter of an unpaid debt," Dring stated gravely, leading the two humans to exchange looks again. Lynx wondered if Daniel had been running up gambling losses and borrowing from the friendly shape-shifter, who was known to be a soft touch, while Daniel flashed back to a fairy tale about a magical dragon who granted women's wishes.

"Does the embassy owe you money?" Lynx ventured.

Dring thumped his tail once and made an apologetic noise. "I see I have given you the wrong impression. The debt is mine, and I wish to repay it."

"Oh. Well, Donna handles the petty cash and she's gone home already, but with all the security we have these days, I'm sure you could leave it on her desk."

"Maybe on her chair, where it will be out of sight," Daniel recommended.

"It is not a money debt," the Maker explained. "The ambassador and her family have done so much for me, taking me into their home and helping my kind reestablish our relationship with the Stryx. I believe the time has come to do something in return."

"You don't pay rent?" Lynx asked.

"Three hundred creds a cycle," Dring affirmed. "It's a fair price for parking space, but as I said, this is not a money issue."

"Why do you say the time is now?" Daniel asked. "Do you want to help out while the ambassador is away?"

"I wish to make a public acknowledgement of my debt, and the ambassador's absence offers the perfect opportunity to plan the event undetected."

"You mean you want to throw a surprise party?" Lynx guessed.

"Exactly. I intend to invite dignitaries from all of the species who have worked with the ambassador, but it seems to me that it would be improper to organize such an affair without the input of your diplomatic service. I want to seek your support and guidance, but I ask you to keep it a secret from your superiors on Earth until the ambassador has departed for her return trip. My experience with your people suggests it would be impossible to maintain the surprise once anybody on Earth hears about it."

"But what about all of the aliens you're inviting?" Daniel asked. "Won't somebody spill the beans?"

"Never!" Dring exclaimed, sounding quite shocked. "Surprise parties, as you call them, are a sacred trust. Even the Grenouthians wouldn't stoop as low as to report on such an event before it took place."

"If you say so," Lynx said, sounding unconvinced. "I don't see any problem with it from the diplomatic standpoint, but I'm not really much of a party planner. You should talk with Donna Doogal."

"I hate to bother her at home…"

"She'll probably come with Stanley for tonight's poker game," Daniel said. "He's taking Joe's seat."

"Wonderful. The two of you and your families will be invited, of course, and perhaps you could prepare speeches. Personally, I'm a fan of Verlock surprise parties, which traditionally include thirteen presentations and two cycles of lectures in honor of the subject, but I also enjoy the Frunge roasts, which put the emphasis on humorous stories. The Drazen boasting feasts are laudable, but you can't count on a mixed group of attendees for singing. Of course, the Cayl..."

"Excuse me," Daniel interrupted. "Rather than a surprise party where people drink too much and have a good time, I'm guessing you mean something like a surprise awards dinner, where the ambassador gets all of the trophies."

"Now you have it," Dring said, displaying his blunt teeth in an herbivore's smile. "Do you think I should tell the guests who agree to speak to bring plaques? Or I could create a series of statuettes for presentation. We could even give the event a name, like, 'The Kellys.'"

"I really think you need to, uh, consult with Donna about all of this," Lynx said. "It would be a shame to go to all of the work only for the ambassador to be made uncomfortable."

"She gets embarrassed by praise," Daniel added.

Dring sighed deeply. "I'm afraid I've been projecting my own ambitions for the perfect night onto an unwitting victim. I shall follow Mrs. Doogal's advice to the letter." He turned and waddled out the door, looking somewhat less energized than when he had entered.

"I hope we didn't discourage him too much," Daniel commented.

"Better to be honest than to put the ambassador on the spot," Lynx replied philosophically. "If anybody knows what Kelly wants, it's Donna. They're best friends and they've been working together for nearly twenty-five years."

"Another visitor," Libby announced. "It's Woojin."

"I've got to run," Daniel said. "I'll be back in the morning if you're looking for me tomorrow. See you at the game."

"Tell Shaina I'm winning my money back tonight."

Woojin and Daniel passed each other in the outer office with a polite nod, and the older man continued on into his wife's temporary office.

"It couldn't wait until I get home?" Lynx asked.

"Haven't swept there for bugs recently," Woojin replied. "This is official business."

Lynx frowned and waved the door closed, and then added the swipe gesture that engaged the lock.

"Something wrong?"

"Our analysts picked up an uncoded transmission from the Empire of a Hundred Worlds to the Vergallian Fleet, warning them about an Imperial destroyer that went missing. They suspect it was either a mutiny, or the officers and crew decided to go dark. In any case, it happened deep inside Vergallian space."

"Why would the Imperial Admiralty send Fleet an uncoded message?"

"Fleet doesn't answer to the Empire, and they aren't officially part of the tunnel network. It was a special deal the Stryx accepted to get the bulk of the Vergallians onboard. The imperial Vergallians have their own home navy for planetary defense, but they don't need the heavy artillery now that they're under tunnel network protection."

"So why would they warn Fleet at all?"

"Our Vergallian division head thinks that the warning was actually intended for all of the species, but the Empire saves face by not having to contact us officially about their internal schisms. After all, it's just one warship among thousands to them, but I'd hate to see what it could do to an unprotected planet."

"I've been attending all of the briefings and reading most of the reports, but I still don't get what it's about. As near as I can tell, Vergallian Fleet is actually better behaved than the Empire of a Hundred Worlds. They just weren't ready for the constraints the Stryx place on tunnel network members, and they were too honorable to sign up with false intentions. Dorothy's friend Affie is Fleet."

"Bork tells me that the Drazen head of intelligence is on his way here to discuss the situation with us. One possibility for why this schism has bubbled to the surface in the last two generations is humans. The Vergallians were getting ready to add Earth to the Empire of a Hundred Worlds when the Stryx stepped in and made us a protectorate for unrelated reasons. We're the closest humanoid type to Vergallians, and they seem to feel that they were robbed somehow."

"Closest humanoid type? Because we look the same and the upper caste women's pheromones work on humans? We evolved on different worlds, and even if our biology has similarities, there must be endless differences at the genome level."

"Maybe," Woojin said, welcoming the opportunity to bring the conversation around to a different subject. "When I took that sick trainee I told you about to a Farling physician, the beetle said that they all refer to humans as Vergallian Lite."

"Don't talk to me about Farlings," Lynx grumbled darkly. "They made me change my name just to dock at one of their orbitals. Did I ever tell you the story?"

"Several times. And you also told me about the Farling drug you accidentally absorbed through your skin that put you in suspended animation for a week. They're far and away the best doctors and medical manipulators among the biologicals, even if they're giant insects themselves. They're the ones who do the interspecies dog crosses, like Beowulf before his reincarnation."

"Alright, so the beetles are leaders in the field of genetics. They hate humanoids, you know."

"They don't hate humanoids, they look down on us as vastly inferior. There's a difference."

"Is there a point to all of this?"

"When I was in the med bay, the doctor asked about my problem."

"Here it comes," Lynx groaned. "What did the Farling quack sell you? Powdered rhinoceros horn?"

"I'm being serious here. I stopped in to his medical shop on the arrivals concourse on the way here from my weekly meeting with our intelligence analysts, and he did a full work-up."

"When did you leave your office?"

"Maybe a quarter of an hour ago," Woojin replied. "I had to wait a few minutes when I got there because he was straightening some guy's spine. His examination of me only took a minute or two." The tough ex-soldier winced at the recent memory of the giant needle that the beetle had used to extract a sample.

"A complete fertility examination in a minute or two?" Lynx asked skeptically. "Did he tell you your fortune while you were there?"

"He says we're biologically simple. Well, my implant translated it as 'biologically trivial,' but I think that's probably a bad usage of terminology."

"I can't believe you fell for his shtick," Lynx said derisively. "It's a gimmick with some species, you know. Talk down to humans and we'll believe anything."

"Libby?" Woojin asked. "Could you tell Lynx that the Farling doctor I'm talking about isn't a quack?"

"Of course. We hire him whenever possible for on-call duty, but he only works enough to cover the rent on his shop and living quarters. He prefers to work independently."

"You hired an insect doctor who sees humanoids as trivial?" Lynx asked.

"I don't think he was talking about all humanoids," Woojin interjected, receiving a glare from his wife in thanks.

"It's rare for Farling physicians to practice outside of their space, but they are held in high esteem by all of the advanced species as the final word in medicine," Libby continued. "Gryph paid a significant contract bonus to M793qK in order to bring him to the station for a hundred cycles."

"What kind of name is M7—whatever?" Lynx complained.

"The information bandwidth of the high frequencies utilized by their native communications has led to names akin to epic poems which translate poorly into most galactic languages," Libby explained. "It would take me approximately forty-seven minutes to offer a rough analog of M793qK's informal name in English. His formal name, updated with more recent accomplishments from the last few centuries, would take days to recite. Would you like to hear it?"

"No," Lynx hastened to reply before Libby could get started. She bit her lower lip and turned to her husband. "I don't think I can go through all of the hormone shots and office visits again, Woojin. The emotional part was even harder than the physical part. I do want to have a baby, maybe even more than you, but we tried the best doctors and it just didn't work."

"The best human doctors," Woojin reminded her. "The Farling offers a double-our-money-back guarantee if he takes the job, and he claims he's never had to turn a human down yet. He said you can do the whole procedure in one visit to his shop if you're willing to wait while he does the tricky parts, and there won't be any hormone shots or nasal sprays. Lynx, he fixed our recruit's brain hemorrhage as casually as you might sew on a button. He's the real thing."

"Double our money back? Libby? Is my husband getting that right?"

"Farling physicians always guarantee their work with aliens and pay cash penalties for any failure to perform. It's a highly effective marketing strategy, and given their bedside manner, a necessary one."

"They don't guarantee results when they work on their own species?"

"Farling physiology is appreciably more complex than that of the tunnel network members, and of most other biologicals for that matter. They have natural immunity to a wide range of pathogens, and given food and rest, they can regenerate limbs and organs to recover from most injuries. But on the rare occasions that they do develop medical problems, treatment is challenging."

"Challenging as opposed to trivial," Lynx muttered.

"Try putting it in perspective," Woojin cajoled her. "If you were a dog, would you rather be operated on by another dog, or by a trained veterinarian? It's the same thing."

"It is not the same thing! Are you getting your comparisons from Jeeves these days?" Then she saw that the hopeful look on Woojin's face was beginning to slip, and she realized that if there really was still a chance, she wanted to take it. "When am I supposed to do this?"

If Lynx hadn't been looking at him the whole time, she would have sworn that somebody had just swapped her husband with a version who was ten years younger. "I think everything will go easier if we wait a few weeks until the ambassador gets back. You're going to make a great mom."

"Just don't tell anybody about this. If it all works out, I don't want our child to be stuck with 'Beetle baby' for a nickname."

# Seven

"Welcome to Manhattan Elegance Hotel," the desk clerk greeted the McAllisters. "How may I help you?"

"I'm Ambassador Kelly McAllister, this is my husband Joe, and my son Samuel. I believe we have a reservation."

"Oh, the EarthCent block of rooms," the girl said in a surly tone, her professional smile slipping a number of notches. She tapped away on an ancient touchscreen and grimaced. "I see it's just the one room for the three of you."

"Yes. There's supposed to be a cot for my son."

"There's a supply closet in every hall, you can open it with your room chit and get a cot. All of the supplies are tagged and we count the towels when you leave, so don't take anything you don't want added to your bill." She slipped two room chits across the desk and informed them, "If you lose your room chit, there's a replacement charge. No outside food or beverages are allowed in the hotel, and room service hours are 10:00 AM through 4:00 PM."

"How can you run a hotel like this?" Joe demanded. "I've stayed in flop houses with better service."

"It's not how we run our hotel, sir," the clerk responded stiffly. "Just the floor of rooms and the conference facility reserved by EarthCent at a special rate which was negotiated by a manager who is no longer with our company. I hear your people gave him a diplomatic posting," she concluded with a sniff.

Kelly decided to ignore the clerk's provocation and turned to her family. "Let's dump our bags and take a walk around the city."

"Your room chits will only work on the color-coded elevators," the girl called after them. "Don't try sneaking into a premium elevator while the doors are open because it won't let you off on your floor."

"Why do people say they like staying in hotels?" Samuel asked, as the family headed for the bank of elevators.

"They aren't all like this," Joe reassured his son. "Sometimes it's nice to get away from home and have your meals brought to you."

"Between 10:00 AM and 4:00 PM, when nobody in their right mind is in their room," Kelly grumbled. "I don't even see a blue-coded elevator."

"It's at the end," Samuel shouted, running across the marble floor. "I've never been in an elevator."

"You take lift tubes every day of your life," Joe pointed out.

"But this is different," the boy insisted. "Libby taught us about them. It's a box hanging in a shaft by a cable, and if the cable parts and the brakes fail, it crashes at the bottom."

"You do know that's not a good thing," Kelly said, watching as Joe inserted his room chit to call the elevator. "How come there's no indicator above the doors?"

"That's to tell you what deck the elevator is on?" Samuel asked.

"They call them 'floors' on planets," Joe said. "When you have so many floors in a building and a limited number of elevators, it helps to know where the elevator

74

car is and which way it's heading, so you can choose the shortest wait."

"And if we can only use the one elevator, it doesn't matter," the boy concluded, having solved the puzzle to his own satisfaction. "That makes sense. What floor is our room?"

Joe and Kelly exchanged looks. The clerk hadn't mentioned the floor, and it had been so long since either of them had been in a hotel that they had forgotten to check.

"Room 3257," Kelly read from the chit. "So the thirty-second floor?"

"It's a pretty big building," Joe observed. "Maybe it's the third floor."

"How come there's nothing on my implant's information channel?" Samuel asked.

"I guess Earth hotels haven't caught up with the state-of-the-art for travelers, and most people living here don't have any need for implants," Kelly said. "Still, you'd think there would be a map or something."

"Ambassador McAllister," a woman addressed Kelly. "I've been looking forward to meeting you in person for years."

Kelly turned and immediately recognized Svetlana Zerakova from the EarthCent Intelligence Steering Committee meetings. The Corner Station ambassador was accompanied by a bearded man and two teenage girls who were identical twins.

"Svetlana. Wonderful to see you. And this is your family?"

"My husband, Anton and my daughters Sabina and Katya. Don't wait for the elevator. We arrived yesterday and I have yet to see those doors open. We're all on the third floor in any case, and the stairs are good exercise."

"My husband Joe and our son Samuel," Kelly introduced her family. "Did you have any trouble with the cots?"

"What cots?" Svetlana asked, as she led them to a fire door that opened onto a stairwell.

"For your daughters," Kelly said. "I wouldn't agree to remain for the whole conference unless Samuel could stay in our room."

"I guess he is a bit young to be on his own," the Corner Station ambassador responded, causing Samuel to blush. "We just reserved an extra double-occupancy room for the twins. The same with the first class cabins on the trip in."

"I couldn't bring myself to spend that kind of money on travel," Kelly admitted, as the two women fell behind on the stairs. "I turned in my first class ticket and bought three regular transits with the money."

"Didn't you request tickets for your family?" Svetlana asked. "I wouldn't have dragged the girls along if the trip wasn't free. They're still mad about missing a party on the station."

"You got free first class tickets for the whole family?"

"Well, I had to threaten that I wouldn't come otherwise," Svetlana said apologetically.

"I can't believe I didn't think of that," Kelly groaned. Above them, a door slammed shut as their families exited the stairwell. "Haven't we already climbed two flights?"

"It's actually four flights to the third floor. I think it has to do with the high ceilings in the lobby and the atrium in the conference center. Have you seen it yet?"

"We just arrived," Kelly replied shortly, trying to conserve her breath.

"The rugs need replacing and the conference rooms are full of those old-fashioned folding chairs. This hotel has seen better days. Which panels will you be on?"

"Uh, I had a request from the president yesterday asking me to host an informal session about alien/human relations for some nonprofessionals they're letting into the conference." Kelly stopped for a moment, breathing heavily, but gathered her strength when she saw that they were only half a flight from their goal. "And later in the week, I'm chairing the panel about how Grenouthian documentaries depict humans, probably thanks to my brief career doing an interview show on their public access channel."

"I always thought it was a shame you dropped that show," the other woman said, pulling open the fire door on the third floor.

"I ran out of alien friends to interview," Kelly admitted. "Are you doing any panels?"

"Drazen/Horten Relations: From Allies to Enemies to Competitors," Svetlana replied. "And I'm giving a public talk on Thursday, titled, 'Making a Career with EarthCent,' though the truth is, I'm a little nervous about that one. Some of the questions I've gotten since we arrived make me wonder where people get their information these days."

"Kind of hard to plan for a career in EarthCent when we don't have an application process," Kelly said. She examined her room chit again, and compared the digits to the cryptic plaque with numbers and arrows on the wall.

"Well, I'm this way, so I'll see you at the opening session if we don't run into each other again before then."

"Thanks for the tip about the elevator." Kelly spent the next five minutes following arrows with room numbers in what seemed to be a circle, until she ran into Joe wheeling a folded cot down the hall.

"Trouble finding the room?" he asked.

"I was getting there. Why? Did you have trouble?"

"I'd still be looking if Samuel hadn't figured out that one of the signs had been stolen. Just remember when you get to the 3240's, start ignoring the numbers and follow the emergency exit signs. We're on the right in the dead-end corridor."

"That cot seems awfully narrow," Kelly commented.

"It has to be to fit in the room. You'd think this hotel was some sort of old space station where space was at a premium. But we didn't come all the way to Earth to spend our time hanging around inside, so it's no big deal. Wave your chit in front of the lock there."

Kelly followed Joe's instructions and they entered the room. "Close the door when you use the bathroom," she called, assuming that's where her son was hiding.

"Svetlana's girls took him to the observation deck. Our floor only has access between 10:30 and 11:30 in the morning."

"Well, we may as well get unpacked and wait for him, since he'll be kicked out in twenty minutes," Kelly said, consulting her decorative watch.

Joe took his toothbrush and shaving gear out of his small carry-on and then threw the bag into the corner. "I'm unpacked. I'm going to pop down to the travel agency in the lobby to see about a sub-orbital ticket to Korea. That tunneling call from Union Station I got while you were saying goodbye to your mom was Woojin asking for a favor. He's authorized me to go by a bank in Seoul and claim some family jewelry that he probably inherited or something. If I leave first thing in the morning, I'll be back in time for dinner. Hey, don't unfold the cot until bedtime or there won't be any room to move."

"All right. See you in a bit."

After Joe left, Kelly took ten minutes to unpack her things, and then retrieved Joe's bag from the floor. It contained one pair of pants, two shirts, and three unopened packages of underwear, a seven-day supply. She wondered for a moment what he had done with his dirty laundry from the first half of the trip, and how he planned to get through the final week in space. Then she went to lift Samuel's bag onto the bed and let out a grunt. It was heavier than she expected, and something jabbed her in the stomach. It turned out to be her father's cane, which was strapped to the side of the shoulder bag.

After a brief struggle with the Vergallian interlocking flap system, she got it opened and wasn't surprised to see that the boy's wardrobe was identical to his father's, except Samuel had also packed his Libbyland toy. Kelly frowned at the little robot, which she had explicitly told him to leave home. Then she recalled the stuffed animal she had not only carried around as a girl, but which currently adorned her dresser back on Union Station, and decided she wouldn't comment about her teenage son traveling with a favorite toy from childhood.

There was a loud sound that reminded her of the low-oxygen warning made by the lifeboat during the brief evacuation training they had received on the Vergallian freighter that brought them to Earth. The alarm noise sounded again, and this time she realized that it was coming from somewhere in the room. Given the limited number of fixtures, process of elimination led her to discover that the culprit was an off-white boxy object on the small stand next to the bed.

"Hello?" she ventured, suspecting it was some sort of crude communications device, like the telephone handsets in old movies. The annoying alarm sound repeated, and she noticed that there was a large button on the box, so she pressed it.

"Mr. or Mrs. McAllister?" a voice asked through the speaker grille.

"Yes, I'm Ambassador McAllister," Kelly replied.

"I'm Tom, the guide on the observation deck, employee ID 2761. There's a young man up here who claims to be staying with you, but he doesn't have a room chit."

"That's my son. There are three of us in the room, and they only gave us two chits."

"Well, he can't get on an elevator without one so you'll have to come get him. Wait, hold on a minute. What? He says he wants to take the stairs, but we keep that door locked. Should I open it for him?"

"What floor are you on?" she asked.

"The hundred and second."

"Tell him I'm on my way."

It only took Kelly two minutes to find the elevator bank, and to her surprise, the doors of the blue elevator opened immediately. She got in and said, "One hundred and second floor."

Nothing happened.

"Oops, forgot the magic word," she muttered to herself, and tried again. "One hundred and second floor, please."

Nothing happened.

She looked for a spot to insert her chit to open the doors, preparing to take the stairs to the lobby and complain, but then she noticed an immense array of buttons with numbers on them.

"Oh, isn't that quaint," she said out loud, and captured the image through her implant. Then she took another picture with her finger pressing the button for the hundred and second floor. Even the elevators at the university she had briefly attended almost thirty-five years earlier had voice control. The car lurched into motion, and she felt her weight increasing as the elevator accelerated upwards. Then she waited. And waited. And waited. After what seemed like forever, the doors opened and she stepped out onto the observation deck.

"Hi, Mom. Tom has been explaining to me all about the city and the gangs and everything. It's pretty cool."

"Gangs?"

"You just have to avoid the ends of the island, Mrs. McAllister," the guide told her. "The middle part is fine." Then he lunged past her and stuck his foot between the doors. "That was a close one. If the car got away you'd be waiting here another fifteen minutes."

"Thank you," Kelly said, and then asked her son, "Where are Svetlana's girls?"

"They already saw the city from up here yesterday, so they got bored and took the elevator back to our floor. I forgot about needing a room chit to get on an elevator, and I really wanted to run down the stairs, but Tom told me it's against regulations."

"Well done, Tom," Kelly said, fishing in her purse and finding a five-cred piece. Then she executed a perfect handshake transfer, silently thanking Thomas for talking her into taking the half-day EarthCent Intelligence training seminar on best tipping practices for all the tunnel network species, including humans. She couldn't remember how she had gotten through life before learning all the tricks. "Let's go, Sam. Your father is probably waiting for us."

"Bye, Tom," the boy said, waving to the friendly guide. The elevator doors slid closed, and he hit the button for the third floor before turning to his mother. "You wouldn't believe all the stories he told me. It's like there are whole sections of the city where the criminals are in charge. Why don't the people just leave?"

"Do you mean leave Earth?" Kelly asked. The boy nodded in the affirmative. "It's a big commitment to uproot yourself and move away from your family and friends. Back before the Stryx opened the planet, there were over a hundred countries, and people rarely moved in large numbers unless there were wars or famines. Most nations had rules for how many new people they would let in, and those immigrants had to be refugees or have certain skills."

"It's much better on the station."

"Yes, but most humans who have left Earth don't live on Stryx stations. People who sign long-term labor contracts to get off of Earth have to live by the alien rules, and the human colonies on open worlds don't let just anybody join. Even the Wanderers enforced standards about who could travel with them, though it was sort of upside-down from what you'd expect.

Turning to a more practical subject, the boy complained, "Why is the elevator taking so long? If you laid this building down sideways, it would probably fit inside Mac's Bones. It's not like it's a long way, and going down should be easy with gravity."

"Your father told me that the controls won't allow the elevator car to get moving too fast because somebody on a floor below us might push the call button and want to get on."

"With us? Ride with strangers? But what if we aren't going the same place?"

"Then the elevator would stop again to let them off," Kelly explained. "It's not like a lift tube capsule that can take you anywhere on the station. This car only goes up and down the one elevator shaft."

"Pretty weak," the boy said. "They should get some Dollnicks to sell them something decent."

"They probably don't have the money. Some parts of Earth's economy are doing very well, but the businesses that have tried to hold on to their old ways often suffer. Now that people can travel comfortably and rapidly in floaters, they don't have to stay overnight if they want to come and visit the city."

"I don't get why anybody would want to visit anyway," Samuel said dismissively.

# Eight

"Would you mind sitting behind somebody else?" Woojin asked the dog. "It feels like you're spying on my hole cards."

Beowulf thumped his tail on the floor three times, paused, and then whacked out another five. Woojin gave the dog a disgusted look, and then mucked his hand without waiting for his turn to bid.

"He did you a favor forcing you out," Lynx said. "If my father knew I married a man who played poker like you do, he'd come out of retirement and insist on a high-stakes game."

"I believe Beowulf is less interested in your cards than the chips," Dring suggested. "It's your bet, Shaina."

"Twenty," she said, pushing two yellows into the pot. "I don't think Beowulf cares about keeping score. He just likes aces."

"I think Dring meant the other chips," Daniel speculated, taking a potato chip from the bowl and tossing it in the dog's general direction. Beowulf snagged it out of the air and moved to sit behind the EarthCent consul.

"Congratulations," Woojin said, as Daniel and Lynx folded in order. "You won yourself a dog."

"Your bet, Herl," Dring urged, to keep things moving along.

The Drazen Intelligence head scowled at his cards and nudged two yellow chips into the pot. "What's your hurry today?" he asked the Maker.

"Jeeves?" Dring prompted, before replying. "As soon as the Doogals arrive, Stanley is taking my place and I'm meeting with Donna to discuss an event for the ambassador's return. You're invited, of course."

"I'll see your twenty and raise a hundred," the Stryx declared, flipping a red chip followed by two yellows into the pot. "If you're planning to meet Clive and Blythe during their Libbyland camping trip, Herl, I can take you to see them. They're near a waterfall, and if you don't pay attention to where you're going, it can be tricky."

"Thanks," Herl responded.

"He's just going to eavesdrop on you afterwards," Lynx pointed out as she threw in her cards.

"Oh, please," Jeeves said. "I can do that from anywhere."

"Call," Thomas announced, pushing in two yellows and a red. "I'll take you to meet them, Herl. Clive pinged earlier and said he wants Lynx and I to be there in any case."

"I wouldn't normally play these cards, but I don't know how many more hands I'm going to see tonight," the Maker said, moving his bet into the pot. "Shaina?"

"Not with the four of you staying in." She folded her cards.

"My mother taught me never to throw good money after bad," Herl commented, tossing in his own hand. "Where are your children tonight, Shaina?"

Dring rapidly dealt face-up cards to Jeeves, Thomas and himself. "Queen bets," he prompted the artificial person.

"We've been hiring an InstaSitter four evenings a week to come in and speak Drazen with the children, even when we're home," Shaina said. "I think it's a shame that most humans get implants so young that they never have a chance to learn an alien language. Combining babysitting with language instruction makes a lot of sense."

"Pass," Thomas grunted.

"It certainly makes a lot of sense for InstaSitter," Jeeves observed. "I'll pass as well."

"I didn't get my implant until I bought my ship, at sixteen," Lynx said. "My dad avoided the casinos with a lot of alien gamblers when he took me on the circuit, but I used to know a little Russian and Chinese. It's all gone now."

Dring fired out three more cards with his stubby fingers, and the remaining players passed again.

"Why did you guys stay in if you're just going to pass all the time?" Woojin demanded. Nobody replied.

Dring dealt the next card, and Thomas pushed in three red chips after pairing his queen. "Queens bet three hundred."

Jeeves matched the bet, and said, "I agree that learning an alien language as a child is mind-expanding. You wouldn't believe how difficult it is to tell a joke in Stryx."

"These cards are a joke," Dring grumbled, giving up on his hand. "I won't insult the two of you by staying in any longer." He dealt a final open card to Jeeves and Thomas. "Kings bet."

"Sorry, Thomas," the Stryx said, pushing five blues into the pot. "I have to go up five thousand."

"All-in," the artificial person replied, pushing his stacks into the pot.

"Can you even go all-in playing seven card stud?" Herl enquired.

"We don't actually have a limit, so you can always bet everything on the table if you want," Dring said. Beowulf barked. "And here come Stanley and Donna, so it looks like I'll be taking a break."

Jeeves stared at his opponent's hole cards like he was trying to see through the waxed paper to the pigments on the other side, which he could no doubt do if he put an effort into it. But he had sworn a mighty oath never to cheat at poker, and after hesitating over his stacks, he tossed in his cards, allowing Thomas to claim the pot.

Paul was the first to greet the new arrivals, taking his duties as host seriously, even though he wasn't playing. "Hey, Stanley. I'll grab you a glass while I bring a fresh pitcher. Do you want anything, Donna?"

"No thank you, Paul. We just came from a late dinner."

"Anybody else?"

"I could manage a Divverflip if you haven't forgotten how to make them," Herl said.

"Since I mixed the last one twenty minutes ago?" Paul responded with a laugh. "One glass, one pitcher, and one Divverflip, coming up."

"Is there somewhere private we could discuss your proposal, Dring?" Donna asked. "Too many chefs spoil the soup."

"We can take a stroll around the hold and stretch our legs," the Maker suggested. "You play my chips, Stanley. It will save Paul the work of cashing me out and you in."

"Fine by me." The former gaming information trader and current chief financial officer of InstaSitter grabbed a folding chair and moved it into Dring's place at the table. The spot was empty because the Maker always stood rather than sitting, in deference to his large tail. "Whose deal?"

"You just missed it," Shaina informed him. "I'm calling five card draw, nothing wild." She shuffled the deck and then quickly went around the table five times, dealing down cards.

"Ten-millicred ante," Thomas added helpfully.

Stanley tossed in a yellow and glanced over his shoulder at his wife and the Maker sauntering off in the direction of the training grounds. "I've been married to that woman for thirty years, and I think she's up to something."

"It took you thirty years to figure that out?" Daniel asked, receiving a kick under the table from his wife. "I'll take three, honey."

"Two," Herl said, carefully extracting his discards from the hand held tightly against his chest. "I must compliment you on your choice of Drazen as a second language for your children, Shaina. I just hope they don't develop tentacle envy, since we have as many idioms involving that appendage as you do for hands." He gave his own tentacle a wiggle for emphasis.

"Three," Jeeves said. "I remember the first time I got up alone on Parents Day in Libby's class to say a few words about our culture. Afterwards, one of the parents said, "Let's give the young Stryx a hand," and I thought the guy was talking about replacing my pincer."

"I'll take two," Woojin said. "I still try to get in a couple of sessions a week with the fencing bot you donated, Herl. I know that at least one other person is using it because I've found it left on the Vergallian style setting a couple of times."

"None," Lynx said casually. Everybody stopped and looked in her direction, and she tried to maintain a non-chalant expression.

"Three for me," Thomas said. "Maybe it's Judith. She was always big into swords."

"She's only been here a couple of weeks, and I noticed the settings changing months ago. It started at Beginner Vergallian and it's up to Advanced Beginner now."

"Can I take four with an ace?" Stanley asked Shaina, who nodded in the affirmative. "Good, then I have an ace," he continued, displaying the Ace of Diamonds. Shaina dropped four cards in front of him, and he added them to his ace to create a fresh hand.

"Dealer takes one," Shaina announced, giving herself a card from the top of the deck.

"If you weren't teaching the children Drazen, I might have suggested Vergallian," Herl said. "It's probably the easiest for your species to pronounce, and it's also one of the richest languages on the tunnel network. I don't think translation implants do justice to the tonal variations that are associated with shades of meaning. Most Drazen business consortiums make a point of having at least one major stakeholder who is fluent in Vergallian."

"Pass," Daniel said.

"You can't pass," his wife informed him. "You have to throw in twenty for the blind."

"You didn't say anything."

"I always play that way."

Daniel pushed in two yellows, looked at his cards again, and shook his head.

"Me thinks he doth protest too much," the Drazen Intelligence head proclaimed, chucking in his cards.

Jeeves followed suit, and Woojin dropped out as well, leaving the bet to Lynx. "Raise a hundred," she said, sliding in two yellows and a red.

"Either you're trying to sucker me into wasting my money, or you've been bluffing all along," Thomas observed. He glanced at the other players who hadn't dropped out yet, and then conceded the hand. "So who do you think has been leaving the fencing bot on Vergallian style, Wooj?"

"I'm guessing it's Samuel. He's pretty fluent in the language, and the Vergallian immersives he watches are full of dueling. And I doubt there's a human male his age anywhere in the galaxy who's better at their ballroom dancing."

"Call," Stanley said, pushing in two yellows and a red.

"I'll see your hundred and raise four," Shaina announced, pushing in five red chips.

"The blind," Daniel reminded her. Shaina shot him a look and added two yellows, after which her husband gave up his hand without another word.

"Sorry, but I'm not going anywhere," Lynx said. She counted out four reds, added two blues, and pushed the stack into the pot.

"I won't tell you what I'm folding," Stanley grumped. "Only that it doesn't seem fair."

"So," Shaina said, observing Lynx closely. "The gambler's daughter is either out on a limb with a long bluff, or she thinks her flush will beat my straight."

"Keep fishing," Lynx said dryly.

"Could it be a full house?" Shaina asked, watching the cultural attaché carefully.

"I love it when she gets competitive," Daniel said, flipping his wife's ponytail onto her shoulder with his right hand. "Come on, babe. It's not like two creds will break the bank."

Shaina looked at him sourly for rendering the blue chips at their true value. Two thousand millicreds just sounded so much cooler than two creds.

"I'll call," she said, pushing in two blues.

"Jacks over," Lynx declared, throwing her cards face up on the table. Shaina looked at the full house in disgust, and then deliberately mixed her own cards into the deck before passing it to her husband.

"So, Jeeves," Stanley said, as they waited for Daniel to shuffle. "Any chance you can hear what my wife is discussing with Dring?"

"Would you eavesdrop on your maker if you had a chance?" Jeeves responded.

The seven other players at the table exchanged looks, and then answered with a collective, "Yes."

"Call it nostalgia, but I don't hear what Dring says unless I'm sure he knows I'm listening."

A few hundred steps away, Donna dropped the casual gossip and stopped to face the Maker. "I heard you want to put on a surprise party for Kelly's return. Something really special."

"Yes," Dring said enthusiastically. "I had in mind a panel of dignitaries. We'll invite humans, aliens, and AI to present awards and to speak about the ambassador's contributions to the tunnel network. Most of the advanced species host similar ceremonies for outstanding individuals, and I hoped to combine the best of several cultures."

"I see," Donna replied, looking grave.

"It's not good?" Dring asked anxiously.

"Well, I wouldn't want to discourage you from doing something you obviously think is important, but it really isn't Kelly's sort of thing," the embassy manager replied honestly.

Dring shook his head back and forth rapidly as if he were clearing his head of the idea, causing his large cheeks to flap. "If you had an unlimited budget and a large guest list to entertain, what would you suggest?"

Donna's heart began to beat louder as she crossed her fingers behind her back and made her own all-in move. "A formal ball with a full orchestra and a grand entrance to announce important diplomatic guests. I checked with the Empire Convention Center, and their main ballroom is available the night Kelly is due back, though we'll have to make a deposit quickly if we want to keep it. There's plenty of time to bring in musicians from Earth, and I'm sure we could get a symphony orchestra, since they always need the money."

"A ball? Like in the novels I borrow from the ambassador?"

"Have you read 'War and Peace?'" Donna asked. She had never read it herself, but she had watched the ballroom scene in every old movie, immersive and miniseries adaptation she could get her hands on.

"An excellent tale," Dring confirmed. "Now that I recall, Kelly strongly suggested that book. I suppose this explains her support of Samuel's dancing lessons."

"Oh, yes," Donna said, tightening her middle finger over her index finger to excuse her next statement. "The ambassador and I have talked about putting on a ball for years." She didn't see the point in mentioning that these conversations consisted of her pushing for the embassy to sponsor a ball, and Kelly displaying an unexplainable lack of enthusiasm for the project.

"No speeches at all?" Dring asked mournfully.

"There has to be a dinner afterwards," Donna said, and then crossed the fingers of her other hand and added, "I'm sure the guests would enjoy listening to speeches while they eat, or we could have a separate room set aside for awards and such."

"A Hall of Praises," Dring supplied the technical term. "The Hortens and the Grenouthians traditionally separate their official ceremonies from the associated social events that way, and I've seen something similar with many off-network species."

"That sounds perfect. And we could divide the workload along those lines. I'll handle the ball, the music, the dinner, and the local invitations, and you can invite the off-station dignitaries and arrange the whole praise thing."

"I worry that I'm asking you to do too much on short notice. Are you sure it won't interfere with your embassy duties?"

"Never mind the embassy, this is important," Donna blurted, worried that the prize was about to slip away. "I mean, I'm sure that an event like this will do more for EarthCent's credibility than anything that happens in the office while the ambassador is away."

"In that case, I'll inform the Stryx to authorize you for all ball-related expenditures on my account."

"Are you sure you don't want to set a budget?" Donna asked, feeling a twinge of conscience as she relaxed her fingers. "I wouldn't want to accidentally overdraw your ready cash."

It was Dring's turn to look uncomfortable, and he blinked a few times before replying. "The Stryx don't let me spend my own money. There's more than enough in my station account to cover a hundred balls, but the debits never go through. Whatever I purchase, the sellers get paid, but Gryph refuses to reduce my balance. He won't even discuss it."

"That's even better, then," Donna said. "Obviously, it gives the Stryx pleasure to fund your station activities, and the more we spend, the happier they'll be." The stroll had taken them around the hold, and they found themselves approaching the poker game in front of the ice harvester from the opposite direction. "Not a word of this to the others, Dring. They'll find out soon enough when the invitations go out." She silently added for herself, "and when it's too late to do anything about it."

"Lynx and Daniel already know I'm planning a party," the Maker told Donna. "They're the ones who suggested talking to you."

"Alright, I'll handle them, but nobody else."

"I'll see your thousand and raise two," Stanley said, tossing three blues into the pot. "And another five thousand if you can tell me what my wife is getting involved in."

"Call," Jeeves said, pushing two blues into the center of the table. "Straight, queen high."

"That's it for me," Stanley declared, tossing his hand and rising from the table. "I had a ten high straight, missed a flush and a straight flush by one card. Dring," he called, addressing the approaching couple. "I'm out of practice and these guys are all sharks." He moved the chair back where he had found it to make room for the Maker to resume his place.

"What's this, Stanley?" Dring asked, holding up the twenty-cred piece which the man had left on the table to cover his losses. "When I asked you to play my chips, I assumed I would benefit from the gains and cover the losses."

"It's a down-payment on whatever that conversation with my wife cost you, so don't refuse it. From the look on her face, I'd say that you just put her in charge of planning the party to end all parties."

# Nine

"Welcome to the first Conference of…" President Beyer winced and stepped back from the microphone as a loud burst of feedback forced the ambassadors, their families, and invited press to cover their ears. "Uh, sorry about that," he shouted from a safe distance. "Can we get a little tech support up here?"

"You've got to be kidding me," Samuel muttered to his mother, who was struck by how much her son sounded like his father when using one of Joe's favorite expressions. "Earth humans can't manage a working public address system?"

Somebody called out, "The monitor is pointing right at you. Aim it the other direction."

"What's a monitor?" the president inquired.

"The speaker on the stand next to the podium that lets you hear what we hear," the same man replied.

"Got it." The president picked up the stand with the speaker, but the tripod legs collapsed into their closed position, so rather than resetting it in another direction, he just laid it on the floor. Then he returned to the stand and blew into the mic.

"Don't do that," the audio expert in the crowd shouted in irritation. "That's an old ribbon mic. You'll break it."

"Sorry," the president said, and then began again. "Welcome to the first…" The feedback was so loud this time that

96

something backstage began to smoke, and the odor of fried electronics drifted out over the crowd. Then the sprinkler system went off. "I always hated keynote addresses anyway," the president shouted. "See you in the sessions."

"Well, that was different," Kelly said to her son. They joined the mob of diplomats and reporters trying to get out of the room while avoiding the spotty coverage of the ancient sprinkler system. "I told them we should have held the conference on a station."

"Don't you think there's symbolic value in holding the conference on Earth, especially when so many citizens are convinced that EarthCent is a puppet government imposed by aliens?" asked a teenage boy at her elbow.

"If I have to choose between symbolism and staying dry, I'll take a Stryx station every time," Kelly replied. "Are your parents in the diplomatic service?"

"Leon, Children's News Network," the boy introduced himself. "I'm covering the conference. You're Ambassador Kelly McAllister. I see you in the news all of the time."

"Uh, Leon. You know what I said about staying dry was off the record. Right?"

"It could be, in return for an exclusive interview," Leon insinuated.

"I didn't catch your last name," Kelly said.

"I only use the one name," the boy replied. "Compounding family and personal names was just another way our previous generations overcomplicated things."

"Oh. My mother watches your network."

"Smart decision. Our motto is, 'Because somebody has to be the adult.' How about the interview?"

"Well, I guess I don't need to be anywhere for the next hour, though I'd like to change into something dry. My son

97

is spending the day with me while his father is running an errand. Shall we meet you somewhere in fifteen minutes?"

"Make it the game room off of the lobby," the young reporter suggested.

"I'll stay with Leon," Samuel immediately volunteered.

Kelly spent five minutes waiting for the elevator, then finally gave up and took the stairs. By the time she reached her floor, the ambassador realized that she was already dry and returned to the lobby. There she stopped at the main desk to ask for directions to the game room, and while waiting for the clerk to finish with a check-in, she over-heard a one-sided conversation between a manager and some executive offsite.

"No, the alarm never went off. Yes, but only three of the sprinklers actually worked, and just for a minute or two before the rooftop tank ran dry. No, there wasn't an actual fire, just a blown amplifier. I don't know, the keynote speaker was probably making weird alien sounds or something. Yeah, all of those EarthCent types are like that. That's hilarious, sir. Can I quote you? 'We took a bath on the conference but they could only afford a shower.'"

"Game room?" Kelly asked the clerk.

"The game room is for our regular guests," the woman responded after glancing at the ambassador's conference badge.

"I'm meeting somebody there," Kelly said.

The clerk grudgingly gestured towards the lobby café, and added, "To the right, follow the signs."

As Kelly walked past the café, focusing on the collection of wall-mounted plaques with room names and arrows, she heard Samuel call out, "Over here, Mom." She turned and saw that the two teenagers were sitting in the café and drinking coffee. A small camera on a tripod with a large microphone fixed above the lens was set up a few feet away, pointing at their table.

"I thought you were going to play some games," she said, taking the open seat at the table.

"That's before I learned that your son was on the cast of 'Let's Make Friends' for two years. We just finished recording a short interview, but I'll bet the executive board will authorize a special if Sam is willing. I just wish I had my card collection with me so I could get your son to autograph his."

"You collect LMF playing cards?" Kelly asked the teenager.

"When I was a kid," Leon replied. "I used to watch it a lot because we never saw any aliens where I grew up in Kansas. We hardly saw any other humans. Are you ready to rock?"

"To, uh, all right. But before we begin, it would help me to have a better idea of your viewership so I'll be able to provide answers they might find interesting. Other than my mother, would you say that your audience is primarily students?"

Leon shrugged. "I don't know. I'm not in the advertising end of the business, but I can check if you want."

"And are all of the reporters your age?"

"I'm kind of old, that's how I got this assignment," Leon admitted, looking a little embarrassed. "We have a policy that correspondents have to be sixteen or older to go on overnight travel assignments alone."

"Why's that?" Samuel asked.

"You know," Leon said. "People can be pretty weird."

"Oh, right," the ambassador's son responded, thinking about what the observation deck guide had told him about the dangers on Earth.

"So how long has CNN been around?" Kelly followed up, beginning to feel like she was the one conducting the interview.

"We started when I was fourteen, so almost three years," the reporter answered, making it sound like a very long time. "We were always talking about current events and stuff over the Teachnet, but after the Grenouthians opened their media center on Earth and all of the big news networks started running cheap archival footage 24x7, we felt somebody had to cover the real news."

"But where did a group of children, uh, young people, get the funding to launch a world-wide news network?" Kelly asked.

"It started with an anonymous donation," Leon explained. "Somebody bought one of the old established networks that was failing and gave it to us. Luckily, they used the same initials, so we didn't even have to change the lettering on the gear. We outsource all of the financial stuff, like selling commercial time, and even though we have an editorial board, all of our important decisions are crowd-sourced over the Teachnet."

"Teachnet? You mentioned that before, but I don't really know what it is."

"The teacher bot network, Mom." Samuel interjected, and then attempted to explain his mother's strange knowledge gap to the reporter. "My mother went to school a really long time ago in a big city where they still had lots of teachers, and my sister and I went to the experimental school run by our station librarian. But Aisha grew up with a teacher bot."

Leon nodded seriously. "Lots of cities still have old-style schools, big towns too, but all of them use the Teachnet as well. The teacher bots are practically free, so it

100

saves a ton of money on textbooks, and gives kids all around the world a way to learn the basics and to keep up with each other. But there wasn't a school within a hundred miles of our farm, so I've always been a botter."

"After living away from Earth for over thirty years, I didn't realize how important the teacher bots had become," Kelly admitted. "I guess I didn't even know that they could communicate with each other. Who pays for the bandwidth?"

"Teachnet is peer-to-peer," the reporter replied. "All of the teacher bots are part of it, so the coverage is global. We just have to keep them charged."

A suspicion about the anonymous donor who launched the Children's News Network began forming at the back of Kelly's brain, but she pushed it aside for later consideration. "I'm sorry that I seem to be the one asking all of the questions," she apologized to the reporter. "There's still a half an hour before the first session, so fire away."

"Great," Leon said. "We've been accepting questions for the EarthCent ambassadors from our viewers for the past week, so let me just sort out the ones intended for you and we'll get started." He pulled out a tab that looked identical to the ones used by Galactic Free Press reporters, tapped it, and asked, "So while your husband is here on Earth, who's running the secret training camp for EarthCent Intelligence agents?"

At the very same instant Kelly began struggling to come up with an answer, Joe was stepping out of the self-driving taxi in front of an impressive building in Seoul. He had been relieved to find that the Korean cab accepted Stryx currency, which hadn't been the case in New York. In addition, the taxi had taken his directions without hesitation, even though he knew that his pronunciation couldn't have come close to how a native would have spoken the address.

The signage on the building was limited to Korean script on a brass plaque, so Joe just hoped it was the right place and strolled towards the heavy glass doors, which slid open at his approach. The lobby was richly finished with marble and shining brass, and the young woman working the counter smiled and bowed in his direction.

"Welcome to Bank Gajog, Customer. How may I help you?"

Joe had made Woojin say a few things in Korean during their recent tunneling conversation, so he wasn't surprised that his implant translated seamlessly, but he didn't know whether the woman would understand English.

"Hi. I'm here to pick something up for my friend, Pyun Woojin. He said he would make the arrangements ahead of time."

"Yes, Customer. We were expecting you. Are you prepared for the security scan?" A device that looked like a miniature periscope with a rubber cup around the lens rose up from the counter and turned in his direction.

"I just look into this thing?"

"Yes, Customer. You will see a small house in a green field. Try to look steadily at the house without blinking."

Joe stepped up to the counter and prepared to crouch to get his eye lined up, but the retinal scanner was apparently capable of facial recognition, and adjusted its own position to accommodate his height. He pushed his eye socket against the flexible cup and stared at the little house.

"Identity confirmed," the woman said. "Did you bring the physical confirmation from Pyun Woojin?"

Joe reached in his pocket and pulled out the plastic 35mm film canister that Woojin had obtained from his wife, who dabbled in antique photography as a hobby. It had arrived in the diplomat pouch from Union Station the previous evening, and been delivered to the hotel. He popped off the lid and extracted the small plastic bag, which had once contained O-rings for a miniature plasma injector, and passed it to the receptionist.

"This may take a little time, Customer," she said apologetically.

The retinal scanner sank back into the counter and another device rose in its place. The receptionist now showed herself to be a technician, cutting the top off the sealed bag with scissors, and fishing out the strand of black hair with tweezers. She carefully deposited the black hair into a small drawer that popped out of the new device, and pushed the glowing green button. The drawer closed, and the machine announced, "Genetic sequencing started."

"My flight back to New York departs in two hours, so I hope…"

"Genetic sequencing completed," the machine interrupted him. "Positive match for depositor Pyun Woojin."

"Thank you for your patience, Customer," the bank employee said with sincerity. "Retrieval from the vault is underway."

Joe was too embarrassed to ask how long that would take after his last aborted question, and before he could come up with any small talk, a large metal box rose from the counter. The side towards him was open, revealing a stainless steel cylinder.

"It's like a safety deposit box or something?" he asked, his familiarity with Earth banks being limited to the time he had gone to retrieve important papers after his parents were killed in an accident when he was a kid. He was hoping the woman would help him open it on the spot so he could retrieve the necklace or whatever jewelry was in there. The Vergallian transportation Kelly had arranged for them included a strict weight limit on non-food personal items.

"Oh no, Customer. The transport cylinder can only be opened by Pyun Woojin. The lock requires an answer to a security question, but only after being activated by a drop of fresh blood from the owner. Any attempts to open the cylinder by force will cause it to self-destruct."

"That's good to know," Joe muttered, hefting it in his hand. He figured it weighed at least as much as the half-case of Scotch he had planned on buying in the duty-free on the way back. Fortunately, it fit nicely in the small shoulder bag he had brought on the daytrip. "Can you recommend a good local place to eat? It looks like I have two hours to kill."

"I'm sorry, Customer, but I believe it will take nearly an hour to reach Incheon Airport at this time of day."

"Yeah, it was a bit slow getting here, but that still leaves me an hour," Joe said optimistically. "I'm a fast eater."

"My apologies, Customer, but didn't the airport staff tell you that trans-pacific passengers must arrive thirty minutes prior to boarding for screening?"

"Screening for what? If I have an infectious disease or something, well, I'm already here and I just came from there."

"Security screening, Customer."

"Are they afraid I'm going to steal their sub-orbital plane? Who am I going to sell it to? Besides, I've got my own space tug back home that could run circles around that thing. Four hours from Korea to New York, and now you're telling me I have to waste a half-hour in the air-port?"

"It's a tradition, Customer. We are a very traditional people. My parents tell me that many years ago, passengers with inexpensive tickets had to show up as early as three hours before the departure time."

"Three hours early for a four-hour trip? You've got to be kidding me."

"They also say the flights took fourteen to sixteen hours back then, depending on the direction of the wind." The woman glanced around furtively to check if anybody else had entered the lobby, and added, "Sometimes I think our respected elders are exaggerating about the hardships of their youth."

As Joe hailed an autonomous cab for the ride back to the airport, halfway around the globe, Kelly was attempting to answer Leon's question about the relationship between station rents, tunnel fees, and the exchange rate of the Stryx cred. The problem was that she didn't really know, but fortunately, Samuel had been paying attention in school and was able to provide a credible answer.

"Thanks, that's how I thought it worked," Leon said. "There was a great piece in the Galactic Free Press about Stryx cred exchange rates into precious metals, but the reporter implied that some of the advanced species may have figured out how to transmute elements, and a lot of our international viewers keep their family wealth in jewelry."

"You read the Galactic Free Press?" Kelly asked.

"Doesn't everybody?" Leon responded. "The teacher bots get the tunnel network edition for free, without the ads. But the paper has some kind of deal with the remaining Earth news services where they trade stories, so the version we get doesn't include the syndicated local news."

"We had a student newspaper when I was in school," Kelly said nostalgically. A quick peek at her decorative watch told her that the interview only had a few more minutes to run, and she realized she would rather spend that time talking about the news business than evading more tough questions. "I was the book reviewer, and everybody used to get mad at me because I only read books published in the nineteenth century. Did you work for a student paper before starting with the news network?"

"I did the crop news for the Student Plains States Journal for a year before CNN launched," Leon replied. "There must be hundreds of regional papers like SPSJ running on the Teachnet around the world, but they kind of suffer from TMI."

"Too much information?" Samuel asked.

"Yeah. It's like every paper has thousands of contributors, even more, and sometimes they end up with sub-editions for the various towns and villages if there are enough kids living there who like to write. The truth is, all of them could use a good editorial board, but how do you tell the kid who writes about fishing conditions in the local creek that his story isn't newsworthy, especially when it doesn't cost anything to include it?"

"That is an interesting problem," Kelly said. "With free distribution to teacher bots, there's no reason to limit the number of stories, but you end up with a paper that nobody can read all of the way through."

"There's a voting system for assigning trust ratings to the correspondents, but most of the writers just don't get the difference between news and diary fodder," Leon elaborated. "That's the neat thing about the Galactic Free

Press. Somebody pretty smart is picking the stories to report."

"I'll tell them you said that," Kelly replied. "It's been really interesting, Leon, but I'm afraid we're out of time. I promised Daniel I would attend all of the sessions in the 'Open Worlds' track. Are you ready, Samuel?"

"I'm going to hang out with Leon," her son replied. "He said if I carry his camera tripod, I can get in anywhere, and I want to see Ambassador Shin's panel discussion on succession politics in the Empire of a Hundred Worlds."

"We always get the most feedback when we do a story on Vergallians," Leon added. "They're practically human."

Not in my experience, Kelly thought to herself, but she knew how young people were often deceived by appearances, especially when packaged in a form as attractive as members of the Vergallian upper caste.

# Ten

"What a beautiful place," the head of Drazen Intelligence remarked. "I can't believe the Oxfords are the only people vacationing here at the moment."

"It's the wastewater treatment aspect," Thomas explained. "The flora and fauna on this deck are from Earth, part of the standard Stryx program of creating emergency nature reserves for biologicals, but its other purpose is functioning as a natural cleansing machine. It's capable of processing sewage from a number of species after pretreatment."

"Yuck," Lynx said reflexively, even though the air smelled fresh and the greenery looked much more natural than the plantings on any of the park decks she had visited. "Where are the campsites?"

"You can't see them yet because of the rocks," Woojin told them. "I've been here fishing with the McAllisters a number of times. Paul told me that originally the Stryx hid this lift tube entrance with a waterfall, but you couldn't get out without taking a shower."

"They moved the lift tube?" Lynx asked.

"The waterfall," Woojin replied. "The lift tubes are part of the permanent infrastructure. Just follow me."

A pebble path led around the steep rock face, and the visitors soon found themselves on the shore of a small body of water, into which a waterfall was plunging. A few ducks looked at the newcomers expectantly, but quickly lost interest when no bread crumbs were forthcoming.

Across the water, a young couple was ballroom dancing. The girl was incredibly graceful, and her partner was a fair dancer, though not on her level. During a spin, the boy caught sight of the visitors and abruptly came to a halt. He waved, pointed upstream at a small bridge, and then ran to get his parents. Vivian looked a bit annoyed that her dance practice had been interrupted, but she walked along her side of the stream to meet the guests.

"Hey, Viv," Lynx greeted Blythe's daughter when they met up. "You and Jonah looked pretty good."

"He doesn't practice at all anymore," Vivian complained. "And I had to agree to play some dumb game with two wooden paddles and ball in return."

"Two wooden paddles for each of you?" the Drazen inquired.

"One paddle each, one ball for both of us," the girl replied. "Like the Dollnick game, but without the mitt and the cup."

"And how have you been enjoying your vacation?" Thomas asked.

"I miss Samuel," the girl replied bluntly. "I practice with the hologram that Marcus recorded for us but it's not the same thing. I doubt any of the Vergallian kids we compete against ever take off two days in a row, much less a whole month."

"Is it Samuel you miss, or the dancing?" Lynx teased the girl.

"Both. But I like him more than he likes me, so there's nothing I can do about it," the twelve-year-old said with a sigh. She stopped and pointed at what looked like a small outdoor theatre. "My parents said they would meet you at the Wetlands Machine display. There are some stone benches and an acoustic suppression field there."

"Thank you."

"You're welcome," Vivian replied. She shook her head as her parents and brother came into view. "I'll have to drag Jonah back to practice now. If he thinks I'm counting the last ten minutes, he's crazy."

As their guide sprinted off to catch her brother, Herl commented, "I'd recognize her as Blythe's daughter even if I'd never seen her before." Then he sat down on a bench and began searching through his leather shoulder bag for something.

"Welcome to our vacation," Clive said, as soon as he and Blythe entered the acoustically protected area. "We ordered refreshments from Pub Haggis, but they haven't arrived yet. I probably shouldn't have told them that whenever they get to it is fine."

"I had a large supper just an hour ago, so I'm all set," Herl said, rising to exchange handshakes with Blythe and Clive. "The Vergallian situation is developing so slowly that I wanted to put off this meeting to the end of my visit, but I wonder now if that was a mistake."

"Are you running late, Herl?" Blythe asked. "Why don't we get started?"

"I'm not pressed for time, though I'll be leaving the station after this meeting. What I meant is that I've received no new intelligence since arriving, so all I accomplished by waiting was to keep you in the dark for several days. In any case, I'll be back for Dring's party."

"Dring is having a party?" Clive asked. "Doesn't seem like his sort of thing."

"It's not for him, it's for Kelly," Lynx explained. "Donna is making all of the arrangements. She still comes into the

110

embassy every day, but she spends all of her time sending out invitations to aliens and going over contracts with Libby for the catering and travel arrangements. I gather it's going to be some kind of formal-dress dance with a meal afterwards. She's saving the human invitations until last, and she said we can read the details then."

"It sounds like Ballmageddon has finally arrived," Blythe informed the others with a wry smile. "My sister and I knew that Mom always wanted to put on a big ball, but she turned down our offer to host one for InstaSitter. Chas couldn't get her interested in doing one for the Galactic Free Press either, even though the guest list would have been interesting. It had to be a diplomatic ball."

"Well, it appears that your mother is getting her wish," Herl observed. "I can't imagine anybody will turn down an invitation from a Maker. We've been tracking the guest list, informally, you understand. If somebody wanted to wipe out the leadership of the tunnel network in a single blow, it would be a good place to plant a bomb."

"I'm on it," Woojin said, in answer to a sharp look from Clive. "Donna already asked if we could supply uniformed foot soldiers to make an impression on the species who will be expecting an upscale event. I figure we'll use the trainees who will be in their last week of the course, plus some analysts to make up the numbers. Since it's on the station, the Stryx will prevent the guests from bringing anything really dangerous to the party, but our people will serve as a visible deterrent."

"We don't have uniforms," Clive pointed out.

"I'll bet Mom said she'd provide the uniforms, didn't she?" Blythe asked Woojin. "And now that I think of it, are you sure she asked for foot soldiers and not footmen?"

111

"Is there a difference? You're right about the uniforms in any case. She said that Dring was buying, so I couldn't think of a reason to refuse. And you're all sworn to secrecy about this if you haven't been already. It's going to be a surprise for Kelly."

"In more ways than one," Lynx predicted.

"Don't be shocked if Mom buys our agents powdered wigs," Blythe said ruefully. "You don't know how obsessed she is with nineteenth-century balls."

"All of the species enjoy a good reenactment," Herl reminded her. "Now that I think about it, a ball might make the perfect pretence to try to get the opposing sides of the Vergallian schism to the table. They're the most dance-crazed species in the galaxy, so I'm sure they'll attend if invited."

"We've been hearing intelligence chatter about the Vergallian issue for weeks, but our analysts can't figure out what's going on," Thomas said. "I read through all of the reports, and it appears that some younger members of prominent royal households haven't been seen in public recently. But whether they've been assassinated, placed in custody, or run away from home, we can't tell."

"Your analysts are looking in the right place, you just don't have the back story," Herl explained. "The Empire of a Hundred Worlds is large enough to support dozens of major factions and conspiracies, and that's without taking into account the twenty percent or so of their population who broke away a few hundred thousand years ago."

"You're talking about Fleet now?" Lynx asked.

"Yes. The Vergallians who didn't agree with the tech-ban system of governing worlds and who wanted to move to a merit-based command structure once made up the majority of the imperial navy. Since they controlled most of the ships, they were able to withdraw from the empire, taking a substantial chunk of the populace and the newer worlds with them. Since then, the Empire of a Hundred Worlds has rebuilt its own navy, and the two entities cooperate in most matters, including weapons technology."

"But I thought that the worlds run by the Fleet Vergallians were still ruled by royal families," Lynx objected. "Dorothy's friend, Affie, is from an upper caste family, but she was far enough down the line of succession to be allowed to leave home."

"Fleet is hardly an egalitarian society," Herl explained. "They do accept the illegitimate children of the upper caste as rulers and commanders, and they absolutely reject tech bans, but their top governmental authority remains vested in queens. Many species believe that Fleet is just a deception that allows the Vergallians to enjoy the benefits of the tunnel network without committing their entire population to Stryx rules."

"So is the current conflict in the Empire of a Hundred Worlds a fight between royalists and citizens who favor a republic?" Thomas asked.

Herl appeared to be shocked by the question. "A Vergallian republic? I've never heard even a hint of such a thing in all my years doing intelligence work. When the rulers of a tech-ban planet in the Empire of a Hundred Worlds lose touch with their subjects, they find themselves strongly opposed in the next war of succession. The battles usually take place according to an astrological cycle designed for the particular planet, but occasionally, an underground movement will put forward a new slate of queens for multiple worlds to push a single issue."

113

"That's pretty much what Keeto, the Vergallian trader who took me in as a child, told me," Clive commented. "But he said that such movements were usually just an excuse for people to join a secret society and hold ceremonial dinners."

"He was largely correct," Herl confirmed. "But every ten thousand years or so, an issue arises that draws enough popular support to create a state of civil war in some regions of Vergallian space. In this case, the casus belli is Earth."

"What?" Blythe exclaimed. "The Vergallians want to fight each other because of something we did?"

"Some elements of Vergallian society feel that Earth should have been integrated into their empire," Herl replied.

"You mean conquered," Woojin said. "I've met several Vergallian generals over the years who say they had infiltrated operatives onto Earth a century ago, and were ready to take us over when the moment was ripe. But the Vergallian plot was spoiled when the Stryx stepped in and gave us early entry to the tunnel network to save us from economic self-destruction."

"The Vergallians see themselves as the archetypes for the five-fingered, five-toed branch of humanoids in this region of the galaxy, and they pride themselves on having built a homogenous empire out of bio-similar species," Herl explained. "The Imperials don't talk about it publicly, but the Fleet Vergallians base their science of evolutionary biology on Stryx interference."

"So that's why the Farlings call us Vergallian Lite," Woojin said. Before he could add anything else, Lynx glared him into silence.

114

"If the Vergallians think that we're all related through Stryx tinkering, why would they want to conquer us?" Blythe asked.

"It's not imperial policy, just a powerful secret society we call the 'Fives.' They weren't particularly upset when the Stryx got to you first because, frankly, you and your Earth were nobody's idea of a prize. But you've become highly visible in the last few decades, and there are plenty of out-of-power Vergallian royals who would happily take over governing a large concentration of humans."

"Why haven't you ever mentioned the Fives before, Herl?" Clive asked.

The Drazen Intelligence head made an apologetic gesture, and then admitted, "It has a derogatory connotation in Drazen. Like saying that somebody is 'One thumb short of a hand,' means they're lazy and likely not sane. I wasn't sure what your translation implants would make of it."

"But the Stryx won't allow the Vergallians to take over humanity," Lynx objected. "Everybody is prohibited from attacking Earth, and the majority of humans who've left home live on alien worlds or Stryx stations. What's the point of building an insurrection with unachievable goals?"

"Since when do stated political aims have any relationship to the ultimate prize?" Herl replied seriously. "Our own assessment is that the Fives are planning to use humans as an excuse to contest a number of thrones in the Empire of a Hundred Worlds. Should they actually win power on some planets, they'll likely make a showy attempt to woo you into joining them, and then forget about the whole matter. It's a way for young royals to get a new round of succession wars going without waiting for their turn."

"It would be ironic if human mercenaries made the difference in some of those conflicts," Clive commented. "There are humans living on Vergallian worlds who have already gone native and acknowledged the local queen as their ruler, so the whole thing isn't as far-fetched as it sounds."

"And where does Fleet stand in all of this?" Woojin asked.

"They're just mad that the Stryx haven't admitted to biological plagiarism or paid royalties for borrowing segments of the proto-Vergallian genetic code," Herl said. "It's all hubris, if you ask me. The Stryx science ships probably fiddle with humanoid genetics according to their own aesthetic preferences, or based on the template of some vanished species that none of us have ever heard of. We Drazens don't waste time speculating about it."

"How do the Fives feel about artificial people based on humans?" Thomas asked. "I've been told that I could pass as Vergallian myself."

"I'm sorry, Thomas, but I'm afraid they are biological snobs," Herl said. "The Fives sponsor scientists who spend their careers trying to recover snippets of genetic code from the fossils of bio-similar species to prove their case."

"But the Verlocks are the oldest humanoids in the sector," Blythe protested.

"They're three-toed," Herl reminded her. "The Vergallians don't believe themselves to be the earliest humanoids, just the best-looking. Their theory is that species like my own, the Frunge, and the Hortens, are all examples of the Stryx trying to steer our evolution in a direction that would yield humanoids more like Vergallians."

"That's insane," Thomas sputtered. "Why would the Stryx want biologicals to look like Vergallians? If anything, you'd think their aesthetic ideal would include a flexible pincer."

"Not entirely unlike a tentacle," Herl deadpanned, waving that member behind his head. "Due to which, we're entirely dependent on informers and technological means for intelligence gathering in the Empire, since no Drazen would ever pass as a native. But thanks to the ability of your agents to mimic Vergallian commoners, you may be able to infiltrate the Fives. In the least, you're in a better position to recruit moles than we are, since your agents could portray themselves as Imperials or Fleet."

"Now that I understand exactly what we're looking for I'll have our analysts go through all of our Vergallian assets again to see if we already have somebody in place," Clive said. "I take it you don't assess any risk to the tunnel network, other than the direct impact on mercenaries and other humans working in the Empire of a Hundred Worlds, should any out-of-season wars of succession arise."

"Well, there's always the possibility that they'll undertake some sort of publicity stunt to attempt to draw attention to their cause," Herl cautioned them. "Your own report about the young Vergallian royals going underground indicates that they may be taking precautions to avoid being placed in preventive custody as the establishment attempts to defuse the situation."

"If their purported goal is to bring us into the fold, attacking a human colony would be counter-productive," Blythe pointed out.

"Unless they make it look like somebody else did it," Thomas speculated. "What if they want to convince people that the Stryx can't or won't protect us when we move beyond Earth or the tunnel network? The Fives could pretend to be pirates and attack one of our off-network colonies."

"They could just hire pirates," Clive said. "Is this the same group that was behind Vergallian Intelligence's attempt to stage phony human elections and convince us to withdraw from the tunnel network?"

"Ah, yes. Your Human Expatriates Election League debacle," Herl mused. "It does seem highly likely, but we've never been able to infiltrate Vergallian Intelligence, so your guess is as good as mine."

"If the bottom line comes down to upper caste families battling over fiefdoms, it doesn't seem like there would be anything we could do to stop it," Blythe said. "Why do you think it would help to get the two sides, or even the three sides, to sit down and talk at the ball?"

"Talking is always better than fighting, at least as long as you keep your eyes open," the Drazen replied. "In my experience, sentients in positions of power tend to underestimate how much their subordinates resent not being the ones in charge. And in an Empire where the royal bloodlines reach back over two million years to the Vergallian homeworld, the opposing sides have far more in common with each other than they do with most of their subjects. It really is a family affair."

Herl rose and stretched, balancing on one foot and pulling the other up behind his back with his tentacle before alternating sides.

"Thank you for making the time to see us," Clive said, immediately understanding the cue that the head of Drazen Intelligence needed to get going. "You've helped put in context many of the stories that Keeto told me as a child. I never realized that the Vergallians took origin myths so seriously."

"Pride is a powerful motivator," the Drazen commented. "Keep me posted if you uncover anything new, and otherwise I'll be back on the station for Dring's party."

"I'll show you out," Thomas said.

"I'll do it," Jeeves offered, popping up from behind a large shrub. "Oh, and here's the catering," he added, setting down a large insulated box. "I happened to be doing a safety inspection of the delivery bot stable in the Little Apple when Pub Haggis posted an order so I volunteered to take it myself. It didn't seem polite to interrupt such an important meeting when I arrived."

# Eleven

"So what do the aliens want from us?" Kelly asked rhetorically. She paused to make eye contact with members of the audience in the Vermont room, the smallest of the conference venues at the hotel. The ambassador didn't recognize any familiar faces among the three dozen or so session attendees with their hand-written nametags, and she decided to proceed cautiously in case the audience turned out to be hostile.

"Everything," a man wearing rough homespun clothing called out before she could continue. "They want our land. Our resources. Our women."

Kelly attempted to maintain a neutral expression, but raucous cheering from the other people in the room made the corners of her mouth turn down.

"And what exactly do you believe the aliens want human women for, uh, Hank?" she asked, reading off his nametag.

"Experiments," he asserted.

"You tell us," a red-faced woman dressed entirely in black and wearing some sort of bonnet over her hair shouted at the ambassador. Her printing was so sloppy that Kelly couldn't make out the name, though it looked like three letters. "I heard this is your first time back on Earth in almost three decades, so I'm sure you know more about it than we do."

"I wasn't agreeing with Hank's thesis, I just want to understand your fears," Kelly replied, wishing she had the words back as soon as they left her mouth. She knew from prior negotiations that telling people they were afraid was a nonstarter for dialogue. "In my experience, the aliens don't want our women at all."

"So it's like that, is it," the woman drawled, her insinuation clear as crystal from her tone. Several of the younger men in the room began looking around uncomfortably, as if they expected aliens to come out of the walls and carry them away.

"I'm afraid we've gotten off on the wrong foot," Kelly said, hoping to avoid the whole topic of the possibility of physical relations between various species. "Perhaps some of you could tell me where you're getting your ideas about aliens?"

"Books," a younger woman answered, holding something up in her hand. Kelly strained her eyes for a moment, before cheating and using her implant to zoom in on the tab, which turned out to be displaying a book cover. The title was, "My Drazen Master," and the image showed a scantily-clad human female with a tentacle wrapped around her neck.

"That's just fiction," Kelly said dismissively, though given the well-known libidos of young Drazen males, it might actually have been an autobiography. "I can't see your name tag."

"Hannah," the girl replied, swiping another book cover onto the tab. "How about this one?" The new title, "Tamed by the Queen," showed a number of near-naked human males posed around an upper caste Vergallian woman's boudoir, including one beaming Adonis who was serving as a living footstool.

"I'll bet you twenty creds that the publishers are just recycling pre-Stryx adult romance novels by adding tunnel network aliens to the artwork," Kelly countered. "I've been living on Union Station for over twenty years and I've never seen anything like that."

"Really?" The young woman displaying the book covers sounded disappointed. "What's so great about aliens then?"

The ambassador was completely taken aback by the question. "I thought you were here to complain about a conspiracy to take over Earth."

"I am," Hank asserted, and several other attendees backed him up.

"I'm here as the local branch president of the ALA, the Alien Lovers Association," Hannah said. "We have hundreds of thousands of members who are so waiting to be kidnapped."

"And impregnated," added an attractive woman, whose nametag identified her as Eve. Kelly would have taken the well-dressed ALA member to be a bank president or a physician had they met under different circumstances.

"This is, uh, unexpected," the ambassador said, struggling to digest the diametrically opposed views of the members of her audience. "Could I ask you to separate into two groups according to your feelings about aliens so I'll know who I'm addressing? Those of you who think the aliens are evil and a danger to Earth could move to the side near the entrance, and those who love aliens and want to, uh, could join Hannah."

There was some grumbling as people got up from the folding chairs and sorted themselves out, but a minute later, it was apparent that the two groups were evenly split. One woman wearing a pantsuit made out of some reflective material remained standing in the center aisle. She raised her hand tentatively.

"Yes?" Kelly asked.

"I don't know where to sit," the woman confessed. "I think the aliens are evil but I still want to get kidnapped."

"Wherever you feel more comfortable," the ambassador replied. "I'm afraid what I have to say is going to be equally disappointing to all of you, but what the aliens really want from humans is cheap labor, new markets, and a species less advanced than themselves to look down on. The special tolls the Stryx have established for Earth's tunnel network connection make doing business here in partnership with humans a low-risk proposition, and EarthCent is working hard to attract more jobs and technology. But if you believe that the aliens are trying to take us over because we have something they want, I'm afraid you're barking up the wrong tree."

"Speaking of trees, what about those Frunge monsters buying up our forests?" a man in a flannel shirt cried angrily. "Everybody knows that they're planting billions of seedlings to take over the planet."

"Despite what you may think, Frunge children aren't planted in forests," Kelly replied patiently. "There's no connection between the trees that grow on Earth and Frunge biology, other than a minor resemblance at the top and the bottom. They've been a spacefaring species for longer than the Drazens or the Hortens, if that helps put their development into context for you."

"The Drazens are acquiring more and more of our agricultural production to starve us out," another member of the anti-alien faction shouted. "They're shipping food from all over the country to a secret factory upstate, and it's all for export."

"I visited that facility just last week, and there's nothing secret about it," Kelly responded. "The Drazens are providing jobs for over four thousand humans and will be expanding operations with EarthCent's blessing. The agricultural capacity of Earth far exceeds the requirements of the remaining people."

"It's an alien conspiracy to depopulate Earth before they invade," shouted Hank, who had previously posited that the aliens wanted women for experiments.

"No, the Stryx won't let anybody invade Earth as long as we're tunnel network members," Kelly told them. "You may have been led to believe that there's a profit for aliens in settling worlds with an existing population, but in order to attract settlers from their own established worlds, developers often need to do a complete makeover. I'm told that starting from scratch and terraforming a lifeless rock actually has cost advantages over reengineering a planet with an existing ecosystem, especially given Stryx rules about preserving native species."

"What do you take us for?" an angry young man yelled. "Everybody knows that EarthCent sold Venus to those four-armed freaks, and that they're using it to establish a foothold in our solar system."

"Who is this everybody you all keep talking about?" Kelly demanded. "The Dollnicks are terraforming Venus for us, not for themselves. They're one of the more adaptable oxygen-breathing species on the tunnel network, but they prefer lower gravity, so if they were choosing a planet in our solar system to occupy, it would be Mars, or maybe one of Jupiter's moons."

"So it's Mars they're after," Hank yelled.

"Please stop interpreting my hypothetical examples as statements of fact," the ambassador said in a tired voice.

"The Dollnicks are terraforming Venus under contract to EarthCent, the same as they constructed the space elevators."

"And who's paying for that?" a man whose nametag identified him as "Truth," shouted.

"The Stryx loaned us the money," Kelly found herself shouting back. "Come on, none of this is a secret. Do you all intentionally avoid checking the facts lest they conflict with your preconceptions?

The room fell silent for a moment, and the ambassador tried to catch her breath and calm herself down. She had been mentally prepared for some crackpot theories about alien domination, but she had assumed that they would at least be based on an honest misunderstanding that she could explain away. Instead, the lottery method EarthCent had employed to distribute a limited number of conference passes to anyone with an interest in attending seemed to have attracted some of the sloppiest thinkers she had ever met.

"How about the Hortens?" one of the women on the ALA side asked, while the anti-alien forces mentally regrouped. For some reason, Kelly found herself wondering if there was a relationship between the questioner's name, Ava, and membership in the ALA, since both were palindromes. "Do they kidnap women?"

"The only people I'm aware of who are kidnapping human women in space are human men," Kelly replied, almost relieved to move back to the alien-lovers topic. "Well, Horten pirates may take women hostage and hold them for ransom, but that's strictly a business thing. I was once briefly kidnapped myself before I became an ambassador, and my understanding is that my abductors were financed by men working at a mining colony who were unable to attract mates otherwise."

"Do you have their contact information?" Ava asked.

"I, er, no. But I'm sure there must be some sort of exchange on the Stryxnet for women who want to become mail-order brides," Kelly suggested. "Does anybody have any serious, I mean, practical questions about alien relations?"

"Everybody knows that the Vergallians are behind the Galactic Free Press, and they're endlessly pushing stories about how the aliens do everything better than humans," the black-bonneted woman said. "It's psychological warfare."

"First of all, you're reading something into the stories that the rest of us aren't. Second of all, the Galactic Free Press is owned and operated by the daughter of my embassy manager. If you look for evil motivations behind every good intention, I'm sure you'll come up with something, but the purpose of the newspaper is to provide humans with information they can use."

"That's not what the Manhattan Post says," the woman retorted, waving a rolled-up paper in her hand.

"I'm afraid I've never read—wait a minute. Is that the printed newspaper I found outside of my hotel room door this morning?"

"Probably. They have the contract for all the big hotels," somebody called out.

"I thought it was an EarthCent prank," Kelly admitted, unable to suppress a smile. "I laughed so hard that I almost choked on the dry bagel this hotel passes off as a continental breakfast."

"Are you denying that the Manhattan Post stories are true?" Hank asked incredulously.

126

"I saved it here in my purse because I want to bring it back to Union Station to show all of my friends." Kelly struggled for a moment with the overly complicated metal clasp that Flazint had designed for the otherwise useful bag manufactured by SBJ Fashions, and drew out the paper. She read the headline out loud. "EarthCent Ambassadors Replaced By Clones."

"So what's your point?" one of the alien-haters cried.

"Do I look like a clone to you?" Kelly demanded.

"Everybody looks like their own clone," the man retorted, and the others murmured their agreement. Encouraged by the support from his compatriots, he continued, "All of us could be clones and not even know it. I mean, except for me, of course."

"Clones don't look like us, they look like each other," Kelly argued. "No, wait. Maybe I'm thinking about the Gem."

"She does kind of look like a clone now that you mention it," the man in the flannel shirt observed, and people on both sides of the aisle murmured their agreement. "Can you prove that you're not a clone?"

"How can anybody prove a negative like that?" Kelly replied in exasperation. "Can you prove that you're not a clone?"

The man turned to his side, scowled, and then squinted near-sightedly around the room until he located the professional-looking woman across the aisle. "Honey. Tell these people I'm not a clone."

"He's not a clone," Eve replied. "I would know."

"That's not proof," Kelly pointed out, playing the role of the devil's advocate. "You could both be clones."

"How about that ambassador who brought her own clones to the conference," somebody else shouted out. "She even had one of those alien names, Zera-something."

"Svetlana Zerakova, and her daughters are identical twins, not clones."

"Are you going to deny the teacher bot conspiracy?" Hank demanded. "Everybody knows that the Stryx supply them below cost to get into our homes and make our own children spy on us. The damn things are never off until the power pack dies, and they refuse to answer questions about any of the good stuff."

"You people really need to get lives," Kelly retorted. "The teacher bots help provide a basic education to children who don't have access to schools, and they save your local governments a huge amount of money on textbooks for kids who do go to school. Next you're going to complain about the special deal the Stryx give us on the tunnel tolls."

"What kind of customer service is this?" Eve's husband demanded. "You're supposed to agree with us and say you'll look into it. Instead you're insulting us, and you even libeled the Manhattan Post."

"Slandered, except I didn't," Kelly informed him. "What that paper printed about the ambassadors is libel. When you lie about somebody while speaking, it's slander. And I'm the EarthCent Ambassador to Union Station, not a customer relations manager."

"This is a waste of time," the man in the flannel shirt asserted loudly. "Let's go disrupt the other sessions like we planned from the beginning."

"No, wait!" Kelly cried, but it was too late. She watched helplessly as her audience streamed out the exit, and she heard shouting coming from the hall when they discovered that the doors to the other rooms were locked. The ambassador wondered for a moment why the president hadn't explained to her that the job was to divert the nut cases into a harmless outlet for an hour, but she had to admit that she never would have accepted the assignment if he had.

"Uh, excuse me?" asked a voice from behind her.

The ambassador turned to see that Hannah and most of the other women who had expressed an interest in being kidnapped by aliens had remained behind.

"Yes?" Kelly asked. If she could salvage some professional pride by keeping this group from adding to the chaos in the hall she was resolved to do it, even if it meant contacting Glunk and asking him if he had any Drazen workers who were interested in carrying off a human woman.

"Was all of that true, what you said, or were you just trying to make us go way?"

"It's true," Kelly replied as gently as she could. "Most aliens aren't interested in, uh, all of that, and the human workers on the alien worlds I'm familiar with live in their own communities. The only exceptions I can think of are mercenaries and domestic servants, and even they have their own quarters. We may be able to breathe the same air as some species, at least with minimal filtering, but we have so little in common outside of the economic necessities that you only see widespread mixing on Stryx stations. Even there, we mainly live on our own decks."

"Then the books are all full of lies," Hannah said tearfully, and made a violent gesture on her tab's screen. The unit blinked once or twice, and then the message, "Your device has been reset to the factory defaults," appeared.

The other women looked equally disappointed, but Kelly didn't see any of them flushing their libraries.

"Don't think of it as lies," Kelly said, patting Hannah's shoulder. "Think of it as poetic license. Just because something isn't so doesn't mean you can't imagine it."

"You sound just like Aisha," one of the women commented, and the others all nodded in agreement.

"You all watch 'Let's Make Friends?'" Kelly asked in surprise.

"It's the only show with aliens that isn't all about war or disasters," Hannah said. "However inaccurate the books are, at least they're not as depressing as the broadcasts from the Grenouthian archives." She looked at her tab as if she was having second thoughts about having wiped out her collection. "How difficult is it to get permission to visit a Stryx station?"

"You don't need permission," the ambassador told her. "You just have to buy a ticket. Most humans who leave Earth for alien worlds sign a long-term labor contract in exchange for having their travel and living expenses paid, but there are plenty of jobs on the stations if you're willing to work. Just keep in mind that it's not for everybody. The stations attract humans who are comfortable seeing, smelling and hearing aliens every day. And if you're spooked by nosy artificial intelligence, don't even think of visiting."

After that, Kelly spent the remainder of the session responding to mainly reasonable questions about life away from Earth and relations with other species. A few of the less angry alien conspiracy theorists drifted back into the room after finding out they couldn't disrupt the other sessions, and the remainder were removed by hotel security for occupying common space and not buying

130

anything from the concession stands. When the time was up, Hannah lingered behind in the room, and sensing that she wanted a private word, the ambassador waited with her until the others left.

"My family all hate everything about aliens," Hannah said in a rush. "When I tried signing up for a labor contract, I couldn't find anybody who would accept me after the background check showed that my brother was arrested for attacking a Dollnick tourist in the street. I was the only kid I knew whose parents wouldn't let her have a teacher bot, and since I left home, it's been a struggle just to make ends meet. Is there any way I could get to a station for less than a thousand Stryx creds? I've seen ads for cruises, but everything costs ten times that, and then you need money for every world they stop at."

"You seem like a hard-working, intelligent young woman to me," Kelly said. "I'm sure you could find work on a station once you get there. Have you looked into traveling on a freighter?"

"How does that work?"

"Some of the alien freighters have cabin space for travelers, but you have to make sure to bring enough food for the trip, since they likely won't have anything humans can eat," Kelly explained, smiling as she pictured telling Donna that she had met somebody who knew less about travel arrangements than herself. "We came to Earth as passengers on a Vergallian freighter and it was really a pleasant trip. Some of those passenger liners are just too busy, and the constant service and the pressure to participate in gambling pools get to be tiresome after a while. Traveling on freighters is more like camping out."

"I am so going to do it," Hannah declared. "I know there's a whole galaxy out there to see and I'm through kidding myself that an alien prince is going to come along and kidnap me. Thank you for everything, Mrs. Ambassador."

"I'm just doing my job," Kelly replied. And thinking about it on her way to the session about trade negotiations with species that didn't recognize humans as sentient beings, she realized that it was true.

# Twelve

"How come Spinner doesn't have to do the stretches?" the Dollnick child complained. It had already struck him as unfair that he had to stretch four arms while the other children only had to stretch two, but the little Stryx simply floated in place and spun around while watching the other cast members follow Aisha through her simplified yoga routine.

"The Stryx don't have to do anything they don't want to," the Horten girl told him.

"Not even eat purple fungus?" the Frunge boy asked.

"Even I don't have to eat purple fungus," Mikey replied in defense of his metal friend.

"I don't eat anything," Spinner finally spoke up, his voice coming out as a nervous creak. "Is that wrong?"

"Spinner isn't biological, so he doesn't have to eat," Aisha said, judging it was time to insert herself into the discussion. "He doesn't do the stretching exercises because metal can't stretch."

"Yes it can," the Frunge boy and the young Stryx said simultaneously.

"Metal stretches," the Verlock girl asserted two seconds later in her ponderous speech.

"I guess I meant to say that stretching wouldn't be good for a young Stryx. Is that right, Spinner?"

"I don't know," he replied. "I've never been stretched."

133

"We could pull on your pincer," the Drazen boy suggested helpfully. "Maybe stretching will help it grow, like hanging from your tentacle."

"Do your parents let you hang from your tentacle, Pluck?" Aisha asked, not wanting to give any young Drazens watching the show the wrong idea.

"My mom picks me up so I can grab the bar in the closet."

"I'd like to try," Spinner said, extending his pincer towards the Drazen child.

"Make sure you don't pinch him," Aisha cautioned the young Stryx. Pluck wrapped his twelve fingers around the jaws of the pincer and pulled. Spinner floated forward and sank downward, so the Drazen boy ended up sitting on the floor on his backside, looking surprised.

"If you just move towards me, it won't work," Pluck reprimanded the young Stryx.

"Sorry," Spinner rasped. "I'm not very good at staying still. Can you hold me, Mikey?"

The boy wrapped his arms around Spinner's metal casing, and said, "Ready." The Drazen boy pulled, and this time, there was very little movement.

"There," Pluck said with satisfaction. "If we pull on it every day it should start to grow, but my mom says you have to begin slow."

"Thank you," the little Stryx replied, and restarted his patented spinning from side to side. "Did that count as stretching, Clume?" he asked the Dollnick boy.

"I guess so," Clume responded after a moment's thought. "Maybe me and Krolyohne should stretch you next time since we're the biggest."

"Force equals mass times acceleration," the Verlock girl asserted.

"That might be a bit advanced for the other children, Krolyohne," Aisha informed the young mathematician.

"But it's true," Spinner said. "Isn't it, Mikey?"

"What's 'times' mean?" the boy asked.

"Multiplication," the Stryx explained.

"I don't think we've had that in school yet."

The alien children looked at the human as if he had admitted that he still required help putting on his shoes, but Aisha welcomed the opportunity to make a smooth transition to the next segment of the show.

"Thank you for bringing up school, Mike. Since we've never had a young Stryx on our show before, I thought it would be a good idea if we all told him something about the schools we attend. Who wants to go first? Vzar?" Aisha suggested, turning to the little Frunge boy.

"Stryx don't go to school," Vzar declared. "They already know everything."

"Do not," Spinner retorted.

"Do too," the little Frunge said.

"Do not," Spinner reasserted, though he sounded less certain the second time around.

"Double do too," Vzar stated confidently.

"Leave Spinner alone," Mike shouted, sensing that his friend was becoming confused

"Children, children," Aisha pleaded. "Is this how we behave when we're trying to make friends?"

"But everybody knows that the Stryx know everything," the Horten girl said. "They made the station and the tunnel network."

"But Spinner is only six years old," Aisha pointed out. "Do you know everything that the older Hortens know, Orsilla?"

"No," the girl replied. "But Stryx are different."

"Am not," Spinner protested weakly.

"We're all different," Aisha interjected, cutting off the possibility of another circular contradiction contest. "I wouldn't be surprised if Krolyohne is better at math than I am, even though I'm a grownup. Verlocks have a greater gift for math than humans."

"Do you really go to school?" the Drazen boy asked the young Stryx directly.

"Yes," Spinner said, slowing his nervous rotation while he spoke. "I'm in Mikey's class in Libby's school."

"What do you do there?" Clume wanted to know.

"Make pictures, learn the alphabet, and sing," the little Stryx responded.

"And Libby teaches us to barter," Mike added.

"Don't you learn to build anything?" the young Dollnick inquired. "My class is constructing a colony ship out of Joopi sticks."

"What's a Joopi stick?" Pluck asked.

"You know, for eating frozen Bizzle juice."

"You must mean popsicles," Aisha surmised. "You should all try to remember that the other children probably haven't heard of the foods you eat at home. What are you learning in school, Orsilla?"

"How to make Joopi sticks," the Horten girl replied. "Our school sells them to the Dollnicks for creds to buy games."

"Good business," Krolyohne intoned.

Aisha heard a muted bell sound over her implant, and she looked towards the assistant director, who was counting them out. "We'll be right back with the new cast after this commercial message."

"The camera light is out," Vzar said, pointing at the front immersive camera.

"Yes, and the Grenouthian standing next to it will count us back in before they turn it on again. This is a short commercial break, so we only have another fifteen or twenty seconds."

"I have to go to the bathroom," Clume said.

"Me too," Pluck chimed in.

"Go quickly. The Grenouthian with the droopy ears will take you," Aisha added. She pointed the two little aliens in the direction of the show's intern, who immediately began praying that the children were already familiar with the equipment in the all-species bathroom. The Dollnick and Drazen scampered off the set as the assistant director counted the show back in.

"Welcome back to the first show with our new cast," Aisha addressed the front immersive camera. "The children are just getting to know each other, and I hope you'll come to know them as well. Yes, Krolyohne? You have a question?"

"For Spinner," the Verlock girl replied.

"You don't have to check with me before asking one of your new friends a question," Aisha told her. The Verlock children were often self-conscious of their slow speech and avoided talking more than necessary on the show, so Aisha was pleased to see Krolyohne taking the initiative.

"How fast can you rotate?" Krolyohne asked Spinner.

"I don't know," the young Stryx replied. "It depends on the atmosphere and stuff."

"Really fast," Mike said, proud of his friend's ability. "Show them."

"I don't know if..." Aisha began to object, but Spinner was already rotating so quickly that the little lights on his casing looked like solid lines and his pincer disappeared in a blur. She felt something tugging at her dress, and then she noticed that Vzar's hair vines seemed to be drawn towards the spinning Stryx. "That's very fast," she called to Spinner, hoping he could hear her while he was going around and around. "Can you show us how you slow down?"

The children were now all leaning away from the Stryx, whose high speed rotation was on the verge of starting a mini-tornado in the studio. Some of the lighter odds and ends on the set slid across the floor towards the whirlwind, and then started circling, like water swirling around a drain.

"Jeeves!" Aisha cried, looking out at the studio audience. "Are you there?"

"I'm here," the Stryx said from behind her, popping himself into position next to Spinner. "He can't hear you because the wind breaks up your sound waves. I'll just rotate in the opposite direction and slow him down gently."

"Is that really necessary?" Aisha asked. "Can't you just tell him to stop?" If Jeeves could hear her through the airflow he was whipping up himself, he didn't let on. The set was buffeted by turbulence, and the slender Horten girl grabbed Aisha around the legs to avoid being sucked into the maelstrom. Then it was over as quickly as it had begun, with Jeeves and Spinner floating motionless side by side.

"In answer to your question, of course I could have told him to stop, but I thought it was an interesting opportunity to demonstrate your Newton's Third Law for the children," Jeeves continued unperturbed. "For each action, there is an equal and opposite reaction."

"That sounds like Wyrlath's Corollary," the Verlock girl said. "Could you show the proof?"

"That won't be necessary, Jeeves," Aisha gritted out from between clenched teeth, inwardly seething at the unnecessary display of force that had disordered the set. "We were just about to play a game, so thank you, and, uh, see you later?"

"But I love playing games," Jeeves objected. "I can fill in until Clume and Pluck return from their secret mission."

"They went to the bathroom," Vzar informed the Stryx.

"They SAID they were going to the bathroom," Jeeves replied mysteriously. The remaining children immediately picked up on the implication and began speculating on where the young Dollnick and Drazen might have gone.

"They could be eating," Orsilla suggested. "I saw a vending machine with frozen Bizzle juice sticks in the corridor."

"I think they're hiding somewhere and we have to find them," Mike speculated, looking around the studio.

"Maybe they ran away because they don't like me," Spinner said, and began rocking forwards and backwards.

"I'm sure they'll be right back," Aisha comforted the young Stryx, though she did wonder what was taking the little aliens so long. They could hardly have gotten lost with the intern riding herd. "Alright. Jeeves can stay until our absent cast members return. We seem to be running a little behind today, so let's try a game that you all know from watching the show. How about the 'I'm thinking of…' game. Do you all remember how to play?" Nobody denied knowing, so the host continued. "I'll start it off. I'm thinking of something rectangular."

"The picture frame on the mantel," Jeeves blurted out before any of the children could even ask a question. "Now it's my turn." Aisha was so surprised that he had guessed correctly without asking any questions that she was momentarily speechless, allowing the Stryx to take over. "I'm thinking of something hard," he said.

"Is it metal?" Vzar asked immediately.

"No," Jeeves replied.

"Is it stone?" Krolyohne guessed.

"No, not stone."

"Is it on the set?" Mike asked.

Jeeves gave a little bob and answered reluctantly, "Yes."

"Good question," Spinner congratulated his friend before asking the older Stryx, "Can biologicals see it?"

"Not directly," Jeeves grumbled.

"Is it making friends with scary aliens?" Orsilla asked.

"Maybe," Jeeves admitted, sounding completely miffed. Aisha almost felt sorry for him after the experience of having her own secret guessed much quicker than she had expected, but the children often surprised her with their insight.

"How did you know?" Mike asked the Horten girl. "You're really smart."

Orsilla blushed bright blue, reminding Aisha of the girl who ate too many sweets in "Charlie and the Chocolate Factory."

"Can you think of something for us to guess?" Aisha asked the girl.

"I'm thinking of something funny," she said.

"Is it a joke?" Jeeves asked. "Is it something that happened?"

"Jeeves!" Aisha scolded him. "That's two questions, and the person who has their secret guessed goes last in the next round. Don't answer him, Orsilla."

"Is it a joke?" Spinner repeated.

"No," the little Horten girl replied with a giggle.

140

"Is it a math error?" Krolyohne asked, leading Orsilla to laugh outright.

"No. Are math errors funny for Verlocks?"

"The square root of negative one is imaginary," the Verlock girl said slowly, and then her whole body began heaving with silent laughter.

"Can we see it?" Vzar asked.

"Yes," Orsilla admitted, staring down at her feet lest she give her secret away by looking right at it, the way Aisha had with the picture frame on the mantel.

"Is it alive?" Mike asked.

Orsilla hesitated over her answer as if she weren't sure. "I guess so, sort of."

"Is it the immersive camera?" Aisha guessed, knowing that children were often confused by the broadcasting terminology.

"No," Orsilla replied, giggling again.

"It's me, isn't it," Jeeves said, sounding surprisingly unenthusiastic about his conclusion.

"Yes," the little Horten girl said, pointing at the Stryx. "You ARE funny."

Out of the corner of her eye, Aisha saw a bunny with a purple stain on his chin fur herding the two missing children back to the set. Clume and Pluck both looked guilty, but they made no attempt to hide their own purple lips, perhaps unaware of the characteristic evidence that consuming Bizzle juice popsicles bore against them.

"I'm thinking of a color," Jeeves said.

"Purple," Orsilla guessed immediately.

"And thank you for filling in, Jeeves," Aisha said, giving the Stryx a gentle push. "Maybe we'll have you back on the show sometime."

"What did we miss?" Pluck asked.

"Spinner started spinning really fast and Jeeves had to stop him," Mike said proudly. "Do you want to see?"

"NO!" Aisha exclaimed, shocking the production crew by raising her voice. "I mean, now that everybody is back, we should move on to our reader's theatre presentation of 'Three Little Shrubs,' using a script created from the famous story book by the Frunge author and artist, Shzcair. We'll return with reader's theatre right after this product announcement."

For once she was happy for the long commercial break which gave her time to regroup. Aisha had worked out the small reading parts for the children in advance and had them printed in the proper languages on plastic slips, which she now retrieved from the props manager. She quickly distributed the scripts, and the assistant director counted them back in.

"I want to thank all of our viewers for suggesting scripts and voting on your favorite choices for our new reader's theatre segment. Because there are seven children in the cast and just four Frunge in the story, the part of each shrub will be shared by two cast members. Mike has volunteered to play the ancestor. Is everybody ready?"

"Creeeeeaaak," the little human boy intoned, sounding not unlike a tree limb bent by the wind.

"This dirt is too dry," Clume said, in the part of the first little shrub.

"This dirt is too wet," Orsilla complained.

"This dirt is just right," Pluck said, shuffling his feet for emphasis.

"Creeeeeaaak," Mike added.

"I will move next to you," Krolyohne pronounced slowly, and along with Clume, made her way to where Pluck and Vzar were standing.

"I will move also," Spinner said, and floated alongside Orsilla to join the others.

"Now we're all together," Vzar read from the script.

"Creeeeeaaak," Mike concluded.

"Wasn't that fun?" Aisha asked. The Grenouthian stage crew all shook their heads in the negative, and the assistant director tapped a paw in front of his mouth, pantomiming a yawn. "Isn't it nice to be part of a story with a happy ending?"

"If we're all rooted in the same place, won't the dirt dry out and lose its nutrients?" Orsilla asked.

"I—maybe there's an underground stream," Aisha suggested.

"It's not the same without the pictures," Vzar said. The little Frunge boy tossed aside the plastic script dismissively. "In the real story there are lots of colorful flowers and I know all of their names. We always play 'Find the pollinator,' in each picture."

"You never made children read on the show before," Clume complained. "I want to play Storytellers."

"I practiced imagining," the Verlock girl asserted.

"Is it my fault?" the little Stryx asked. "Did you make us read a story because my imagination is bad?"

"No, no, Spinner," Aisha protested. "Reader's theatre is just something we wanted to try out. It was on the schedule before you joined."

"Can we play Storytellers?" the bright Horten girl asked.

"I don't have a beginning prepared," Aisha protested.

"I can do it," Orsilla offered, rushing ahead on her own. "Once upon..."

"A TIME," the other little children shouted happily.

"There was a giant space monster on Union Station," the Horten girl continued, her eyes wide and shining. Aisha groaned to herself. She liked to start Storytellers on a happy note, though the children always found a way to introduce scary aliens and witches. A muted ping on her implant told her that a commercial break was pending, but when she glanced at the assistant director for a count-down, she was stunned to see him waving it off. Aisha sighed and pointed at Clume to take the next turn.

"It had long tentacles and giant teeth, and it was all yellow," the Dollnick boy elaborated. "And it crawled through the station looking for little children to eat."

"But the monster didn't find any children because they were all hiding," Aisha amended, before pointing at Krolyohne in the hope that the Verlock girl would exile the tentacled beast to outer space.

"So the monster got really angry and it began tearing the station apart," Krolyohne said, so excited by the idea that she spoke almost as quickly as the others.

"But the Stryx didn't like having their station torn apart," Aisha contributed, and pointed at Spinner for him to continue.

The little Stryx hesitated for a moment, turning rapidly in one direction and then the other, before saying, "So Gryph sent Jeeves to fight the monster."

Aisha sagged. The last thing she wanted in Storytellers was a pitched battle, but the show was going out live, or at least, live with a delay, so she pointed resignedly at Pluck.

"But the monster was soooo big that it grabbed Jeeves in its tentacles," the little Drazen boy said.

"And it tried to stretch Jeeves to help him grow," Aisha suggested hopefully, before pointing at Vzar.

"But Jeeves didn't stretch, so the monster ate him up in one gulp," the little Frunge said, tickled by the idea of a monster eating an all-powerful Stryx.

"Oh, no," Aisha cried, horrified by the direction of the story. "Can't we have a happy ending, Mike?"

The boy could see that Aisha was upset, and he felt bad for the Stryx, so he completed the story with, "But the monster got so sick from eating Jeeves that it died. And we all lived happily ever after."

Another ding over her implant informed Aisha that the Grenouthians were finally getting to the commercial. The assistant director gave her the thumbs up. Station-wrecking monsters were always ratings boosters on children's shows. She caught something moving in her peripheral vision, and as Jeeves skirted the set on his way to the exit, she distinctly heard him mutter something about knowing where he wasn't wanted.

"We're back, but we're almost out of time," Aisha announced when the light on the front immersive camera went live. "Is everybody ready to sing our theme song?" The children all nodded, and the assistant director cued the music.

*Don't be a stranger because I look funny,*
*You look weird to me, but let's make friends.*
*I'll give you a tissue if your nose is runny,*
*I'm as scared as you, so let's make friends.*

"Some of you really do look funny," Orsilla said with a giggle after the song ended.

"Having just two arms is weird," Clume declared.

"I don't think I'm scared anymore," Spinner added, just before the light on the front immersive camera winked out.

"That's a wrap," the assistant director called. "Great chemistry with this cast. I see a bonus in my future."

# Thirteen

"Do any of the panel members want to offer an example of a Grenouthian documentary that makes fun of humans?" Kelly asked.

The room was large, but after the sound equipment failure at the keynote address, the presenters in the individual sessions had all decided that discretion was the better part of valor, and defaulted to speaking loudly. An unexpected benefit of the no-tech approach was that the audiences stayed as quiet as possible to increase their chances of hearing what the speakers were saying. It also saved two minutes at the start of every session during which presenters would normally have to beg the audience to take seats closer to the front.

"The one about Earth's economy before the Stryx stepped in," Ambassador Monaro offered from Kelly's left at the panel table. "What was it called again?"

"Fool's Gold," Ambassador Enoksen answered from two seats away on Kelly's other side. "My own favorite was the one about human democracy through the ages, though the title seems to have escaped me."

"A Thousand Monkeys," Ambassador Fu said.

"Our station librarian recommended that documentary to me," Kelly admitted. "It wasn't anywhere near as insulting as the one about the history of human hygiene."

"The Well in the Cesspool," Ambassador Enoksen contributed. "You have to admit that the bunnies have a talent for coming up with catchy titles."

"So the question for our panel members, which I'll open to the audience afterwards, is why do the Grenouthians make fun of us?" Kelly turned first to the colleague who she already knew from the intelligence steering committee. "Ambassador Fu?"

"Because they can," he answered without hesitation. "Let's face the facts. By the time the advanced species joined the tunnel network, they knew that bathing doesn't kill you, that sacrificing children won't make it rain, and that piling on debt is just robbing your own future."

"So did we, except for the last one about the debt," somebody in the audience objected.

"But the aliens figured these things out tens or hundreds of thousands of years before developing interstellar travel and being invited to join the tunnel network, so the source materials for a historical documentary no longer existed," Ambassador Fu pointed out. "By bringing us onto the tunnel network through their remedial program, the Stryx short-circuited our natural development. What might have become forgotten episodes from our pre-history are instead our recent past."

"I hadn't thought of that," Kelly said. "So even something like the Hortens creating a cosmetic product that accidentally altered the genome of their entire species isn't as attractive to the Grenouthian producers as, say, humans in the last century building wider and wider roads that resulted in bigger and bigger traffic jams."

"Highways to Hell," Ambassador Fu informed her, showing that he had seen the recent horror documentary. "Not only were the bunnies able to obtain cheap or free imagery of road construction and the traffic jams in major cities, they were able to conduct interviews with elderly survivors who remembered abandoning cars and walking home."

"I actually did see a rerun of an old Grenouthian documentary about the genetic change the Hortens accidentally inflicted on themselves, but it was all talking heads and recreations," Ambassador Enoksen commented. "I don't think it did much in the ratings."

"So again, for the panel," Kelly said. "Does anybody believe that the sole motivation for the Grenouthians in making these documentaries is the low-cost availability of content, or do you think they are killing two birds with one stone and intentionally embarrassing us?"

"The Grenouthians are not an aggressive species, although they can be quite intimidating in person because of their size," Ambassador Monaro replied. "Even though it may seem that they are endlessly picking on us by exposing the mistakes and tragedies of our history, in recent years they have been providing Earth broadcasters with extensive archival coverage of all of the alien screw-ups for the last few million years."

"Not to mention broadcasting 'Let's Make Friends,'" Ambassador Fu added.

"So it would appear that those of us on the panel don't see the documentaries as an attack, but rather as a business model," Kelly said. "What do people in the audience think? Yes, Mr. President?"

The EarthCent president rose to his feet in the front row, turned to face the audience, and began speaking in a loud voice. "Our public relations director, Hildy Greuen, has been running—what do you call it, Hildy?"

"Regression analysis. It's a method of standard statistical modeling," Hildy supplied the answer in her normal tone.

"Regression modeling," the president continued loudly. "It turns out that alien tourism to Earth peaks after popular documentaries, even the ones about poor service in the hotels or xenophobic street gangs attacking aliens. In other words, it appears that all publicity is good publicity."

"I never said that," Hildy exclaimed, raising her voice, but the president shushed her and went on.

"A number of interesting proposals have recently come across my desk from expatriate humans looking for funding to improve humanity's image in their own locales. I'm particularly attracted to an idea conceived by a woman who worked for years covering the human diaspora for a Grenouthian news service. She suggested piggybacking on the documentaries with humorous rebuttals."

"So when they rebroadcast 'Fool's Gold,' we would be ready with a sort of an infomercial about doing business with Earth today?" Ambassador Enoksen asked.

"Exactly, but keeping it light," the president replied. "Nobody likes a species without a sense of humor. We have to show that we can take a joke."

"Maybe the tagline could be, 'Sure, it's another pyramid scheme, but this is your opportunity to get in at the bottom,'" somebody in the audience called out.

After the laughter died down enough to allow her to be heard without really shouting, Kelly suggested, "That might be a little too light. Is there any way we can get advance notice of the documentaries before they come out?"

"Don't you get a program guide on Union Station?" Ambassador Monaro asked in surprise.

"Oh, I forgot. I don't really watch much of anything," Kelly admitted. "I'm more of a reader."

"So why are you chairing the panel on Grenouthian broadcast documentaries?" a woman called out from a seat near the side exit. She had an official press pass around her neck, though Kelly didn't recognize the network.

The president turned to address the correspondent. "Ambassador McAllister conducted the most watched interview in the history of the Grenouthian network, and it's not a coincidence that she shares the same family name as Aisha McAllister."

"Oops," the reporter said apologetically. "I just got roped into this gig this morning because nobody else wanted to do it, and I had to ask a question to get credit. I usually cover cage fighting and floater racing."

"How far ahead of time do the Grenouthians announce new documentaries?" Kelly asked. She figured that she'd already exposed her ignorance, so she may as well get her money's worth.

"It varies," Ambassador Monaro explained. "Each season is announced in advance, so figuring the Grenouthian year at around five cycles, or a little less than ten months, there's plenty of notice to prepare something."

"And we would buy time during the documentary to run pro-Earth infomercials," Ambassador Fu surmised, directing his words not at Kelly, but towards the audience.

"Exactly," the president confirmed. "Hildy recommends getting enough of a jump on each documentary to be able to test our infomercials with target groups of aliens. What, Hil?"

The public relations director decided she'd had enough of playing puppeteer to a life-size president doll, and stood up to talk. "As long as we have a room full of ambassadors, I want to point out that the most cost-effective place to test our message with alien audiences is on Stryx stations, where the target groups are all present in large numbers. If anybody is interested in participating, please let me know. There's no need for one embassy to carry the whole load. If everybody took responsibility for a single species, that would be great."

Kelly waited a minute while the public relations director took the names of volunteers, and then continued. "Alright, then. Maybe the title of this session was misleading, since we all seem to be on the same page about the Grenouthians."

"How about cost?" Ambassador Zerakova called out from the audience. "What does a spot on the Grenouthian network go for?"

"The Grenouthians broadcast everywhere the Stryxnet reaches, and they also sell content to off-network species through various arrangements, including delivery of physical media to distribution points by jump-ship," Hildy explained. "You have to keep in mind that most alien audiences living on planets either don't have implants or haven't programmed them to translate any human languages. We would only advertise to a small segment of the watchers."

"So a tourism infomercial could target aliens who can breathe Earth's atmosphere," somebody suggested.

"And what would that cost?" Ambassador Zerakova followed up on her earlier question.

"A lot," Hildy hedged. "We're actually hoping to convince some of the aliens now doing business on Earth to participate in the infomercials and share in the broadcast costs. I've broached the subject with a couple of the Drazen and Dollnick entrepreneurs who are doing well here, and

152

as long as we can make a good business case for the advertising, I think they'll come on board."

"Could you give us a ballpark figure for, say, reaching just the Hortens?" another ambassador asked.

"All of the alien species on the tunnel network vastly outnumber us, you know," Hildy said, faltering slightly. "And the final cost depends on the instantaneous viewership, which the Grenouthians adjust for through use of some sort of advanced polling technology."

"You're talking millions of creds, aren't you?" Ambassador Zerakova asked.

Hildy grimaced and made a small gesture pointing upwards.

"Tens of millions?"

"Maybe," Hildy said, though her tone made it clear that she expected it would be more.

"So when you were talking about asking the local alien businessmen to share in the costs, you really meant convincing them to pay for the whole thing," Svetlana said.

"Pretty much," Hildy admitted. "Earth never had an advertising platform that reached trillions of sentients. The charges are actually very reasonable on a per viewer basis."

"You had me excited about that idea for a moment," Ambassador Fu grumbled. "You're talking about ads that cost more than EarthCent's budget forever."

"How about barter?" somebody suggested.

"Barter is better," a number of ambassadors who were posted to Stryx stations responded reflexively.

"What do we have that the Grenouthians want?" Kelly asked.

"Source material for more documentaries," the president suggested. "It's really a big business for them."

"But haven't they already bartered for copies of all of Earth's major media libraries in return for licensing their own archival content?" one of the local EarthCent staff asked.

A number of groans were heard around the room, along with something that sounded like, "Damn bunnies outsmarted us again."

Kelly spotted a young man with his hand up. "Yes, Leon?"

"The documentaries about Earth are educational and I think that everybody should watch them, but the archival footage of alien wars that's taken over the mainstream news networks is totally negative," the teenage correspondent pointed out. "You can hardly turn around in this city without seeing a holographic projection of super-violent alien stuff from who knows where or how long ago. At least somebody should make sure that little kids aren't seeing it."

"I'm afraid I don't know anything about what the Earth networks were broadcasting before the Grenouthians opened up shop here and began supplying content," Kelly said. "Was it really better three or four years ago?"

"I was kind of busy with my education back then, but I think it was mainly violent stuff about humans," Leon admitted.

"So let me offer you Hobson's choice, young man," Ambassador Fu stated. "Would you prefer around the clock broadcasts of alien violence from history, or continual reporting on human violence from the present?"

"Hobson's choice is something or nothing," the teenage reporter retorted. "Choosing between human violence and alien violence is more of a dilemma."

"You're correct, of course, but you're also avoiding the question," Ambassador Fu replied.

"Well, human violence may seem more real to kids, and in that way more scary," Leon said thoughtfully. "But seeing advanced species fighting endless wars destroys hope for the future, and that's every child's most precious possession."

There was a long silence after this answer, before the president remarked quietly, "From the mouths of babes."

"Did anybody else see the Grenouthian documentary about balls last night?" Ambassador White asked from the audience. "It was on around two in the morning, but I still haven't gotten over my tunnel-lag, so I was up."

"That's why I wear sunglasses inside," somebody near her commented.

"Did you say a documentary about balls?" Kelly asked. "Like, ping-pong balls, and beach balls, and..."

"Dancing balls," Ambassador White interrupted. "I bring it up because from start to end, it was the most complimentary documentary about humans that I've ever seen."

"That it was," another EarthCent diplomat with bags under his eyes confirmed. "And the weird thing was how many important Grenouthians had cameo appearances, talking about how much they would love to attend a human ball if they ever had the opportunity. You'd think if it was that important to them, they'd just throw their own."

"But where did they get the material?" Kelly asked. "Nobody has balls anymore, unless you're talking about some rich people playing make-believe in resort towns. I imagine the Russian czars or the English royals might have allowed an early movie maker to document a ball, but that would have been grainy black-and-white film without the sound."

"The production values weren't quite up to par for the Grenouthians, almost like it was a rush job," Ambassador White replied. "I think I recognized most of the ball scenes from pre-immersive movies, and there was a segment about masquerade balls that used extended excerpts from the recent remakes of 'Romeo and Juliet' and 'Phantom of the Opera.' I've never seen the Grenouthians treat any documentary subject with such a positive bias before."

"Could the Grenouthians have been reacting to news reports of this conference, or even preemptively trying to control the results of this session?" Ambassador Monaro asked. "I know I checked the program guide for upcoming documentaries before leaving the station for Earth, and there weren't any new releases scheduled this week."

"But why balls?" Kelly asked. "If the bunnies wanted to throw us a bone, they could have produced a documentary about our gardening. I've met with Grenouthian businessmen from the station who have visited Earth, and the one thing they all agreed on was the sculpted gardens. I remember one bunny in particular who got lost in a labyrinth at some restored country estate and said he hired the designer to create a maze on their recreational deck."

"I'm more interested in knowing why they would do anything to get on our good side," Ambassador Fu said. "I'd like to say that I get along well with the Grenouthian ambassador on my station, but the truth is, I don't even know his name. I've just been calling him 'Ambassador' since I was appointed."

"Are the Grenouthians concerned about the Vergallian rumors?" somebody asked. "We may not have any significance as military allies, but we probably look just like

Vergallians to a giant bunny, so they might think we have good intelligence sources in the Empire of a Hundred Worlds."

"If the Grenouthian ambassador I know wanted us to share information about the Vergallians, he would summon me to their embassy and demand that I provide it," Ambassador Fu responded.

"Maybe they're worried about competition," Ambassador Enoksen suggested. "The Grenouthians probably assume that EarthCent has some control over the human media, so maybe they're buttering us up before asking that we rein in the Galactic Free Press."

"The total readership of the paper isn't even a rounding error compared to the viewership of the Grenouthian networks," Kelly pointed out. "You're talking about hundreds of millions versus I don't know how many trillions."

A man with a press pass identifying him as a Galactic Free Press correspondent got up and said, "We get along fine with the Grenouthians. In fact, my editor said that they're paying half of our expenses for this conference in return for sharing in our coverage. They didn't send any of their own correspondents."

"So we're not important enough for the Grenouthians to send a reporter to our first Conference of Ambassadors, yet they produced a documentary to get on our good side?" Ambassador Fu asked. "Something doesn't add up."

"I think the reason the Grenouthians skipped covering the conference themselves is that they didn't expect any good visuals," the reporter said. "The galaxy doesn't need to see immersive footage of diplomats sitting around and talking."

"Especially human diplomats," Ambassador White contributed from her seat next to the reporter.

"What does EarthCent Intelligence make of the Vergallian situation?" Leon asked.

"That's, uh, pretty far off topic for this session," Kelly replied. "Does anybody have any more questions about the Grenouthian documentaries?"

"What does EarthCent Intelligence make of the Grenouthian documentaries," the Children's News Network correspondent followed up immediately.

"They liked the one about human spies in the nineteenth and twentieth centuries," Kelly said, hoping to avoid getting dragged into a discussion about classified intelligence. "You wouldn't believe how much money the old Earth governments used to spend on espionage, especially the hardware. Those black budgets would have bought a lot of commercial time on the Grenouthian network."

# Fourteen

"I would have preferred to just stay home for the week-end, but the spa certificate was a gift from the production crew, and you know how sensitive Grenouthians can be," Aisha explained to Dorothy. "It must have cost them a fortune since it's the beginning of a major alignment."

"Which species?"

"Grenouthians, Vergallians, Drazens and humans all start the weekend within a few hours of each other, and the Frunge, Hortens and Verlocks are on holiday equivalents already. Libby said that the last time so many species took a few days off at the same time was at Carnival."

"Don't forget to feed Beowulf," Paul said, coming out of the kitchen with Fenna. "I already took care of watering the plants, so don't give them any even if you think they look dry or you'll just rot their roots. The campground is empty, and Gryph will route any incoming requests for towing to the Dollnick small ship facility."

"We'll be at the Gold Sash Spa on the Grenouthian park deck if you have an emergency," Aisha added. "Please use up all the leftovers or they'll be spoiled by the time we get back."

"Alright already. You guys talk like I've never been here alone before."

"Have you?" Aisha asked.

"Sure. Like the time when..." Dorothy trailed off and stared into the distance, trying to remember. "Maybe I haven't, but Beowulf is here, and Dring is just across the hold."

"I haven't seen Dring in a couple of days," Paul said. "Anyway, don't drink all the beer unless you're ready to brew a new batch."

"Have a good time." Dorothy stooped over and gave Fenna a kiss. "I'm going to miss you." She stood at the top of the ice harvester's ramp, watching until the three figures exited Mac's Bones, and then she pinged Flazint.

"What is it?" the Frunge girl's sleepy voice said in Dorothy's head.

"I have Mac's Bones to myself, and it's a major alignment weekend," Dorothy said out loud, too excited to subvoc for the implant. "Like, everybody is off."

"Fashion Flash?" Flazint asked, coming wide awake.

"You start getting the word out. I'll ping Affie and start lining up extra models to wear our products."

"Should I put it on the Open Circuit?"

Dorothy hesitated for a moment. The Open Circuit was the social calendar maintained by Open University students, who she knew numbered at least in the tens of thousands. But she doubted that more than a tiny fraction of the students were at loose ends on a major calendar alignment, and it wasn't like she had to feed them a sit-down dinner.

"Sure, list it as a flash industrial dance event, starting in, say, four hours. Do you know anybody who has a band that's available?"

"It's awfully short notice to get a band," the Frunge girl cautioned her.

"I'll try the Horten group that their ambassador's son sings in. They do cross-species, and David sort of likes them."

"Good luck. I've got to do something with my hair vines, but I'll see you in a couple of hours."

As soon as Flazint broke the connection, Dorothy pinged Affie and repeated the story.

"Great timing," said the third member of the design team for SBJ Fashions. "I'm at a Vergallian thing, but everybody is talking Empire politics like there's about to be a civil war or something, which is just silly. I'll spread the word, and if you can't find any bands, I can bring my player. Have you pinged Jeeves yet?"

"I haven't even pinged David yet, though I know he's working until late. I'm going to try Chance now, and maybe she'll bring Thomas and help get the dancing started. Don't worry about lugging your player. My dad has all sorts of audio equipment in the ice harvester, and I can always ask Libby to pipe something in."

"See you soon."

"Libby? Can you put me in touch with the Horten ambassador's son, Mornich?

"Just a moment, I'll see if he's free."

Dorothy was practically hopping from one foot to the other as she waited. Looking around Mac's Bones, she could see at least a dozen things that needed to be done, not to mention changing the lighting. She breathed a sigh of relief when she remembered that her father had put an all-species bathroom at the edge of the training camp when EarthCent Intelligence started hiring alien trainers. It would be best to set up for the party between the training area and the ice harvester.

"What?" a Horten youth asked in her head.

"This is Dorothy, the EarthCent ambassador's daughter."

"The station librarian told me," Mornich replied curtly. "Why are you pinging me?"

"Our business is hosting an industrial dance party in, uh, three and a half hours. I really liked your band and I wondered if you were available."

"Is Three and a Half Hours the name of a new club?" the Horten asked, sounding intrigued.

"It's a time, as in, uh, two hundred and ten minutes from now," Dorothy replied.

"Is this a prank ping? You aren't supposed to identify yourself."

"It'll be fun. It's a flash fashion thing, you know?"

"Like, you're going to be modeling clothes and pretending that it's a party?"

"It will be a party, with clothes. You know there will be more girls than boys," she added desperately. "And we design cross-species. Our first product line was Horten hats."

"What's it pay?"

"Double your usual rate," Dorothy offered, not having a clue how much bands earned for an evening.

"We usually play for drinks," the Horten admitted. "Look, I'm open, and if there are going to be models dancing, I can probably get most of the guys. But we've been using club gear for the last couple of years rather than buying equipment and hauling it around, so we only own our instruments and mics."

"Can you rent what you need? Just charge everything to SBJ Fashions. Give them my name."

"How about food?"

"Order whatever you want, same way."

"Deal. Hey. Where does everything get delivered?"

"Mac's Bones. I'll be here to tell them where to put things."

"The human spy camp?"

"Everybody is off this weekend," the girl explained.

"Cool. I'll see you in a while."

Dorothy continued to burn up her implant, pinging everybody she could think of who might help make the fashion dance party a success on short notice. Even though the very name implied spontaneity, all of the flash events she had attended had the feel that somebody had gone to a lot of work to make everything look casual.

A couple of Hortens arrived with a string of bots carrying all sorts of road cases, and she directed them to set up for the band on the platform that EarthCent Intelligence used for staging holo training. The caterer David recommended showed up with several enormous cooler chests of cold cross-species fruit platters and finger food. Dorothy had to shoo Beowulf into the ice harvester before the caterers would agree to bring out a half-dozen folding tables from the storage area in the back, but it took them less than five minutes to lay out a gorgeous spread.

"There's that much again in the coolers under the tables," the Gem supervisor told her. "If you start running low, just ping us and we'll bring another load."

"Thank you," Dorothy called after the clones as they rushed off to their next job.

Flazint arrived with her hair vines done up on a fancy trellis, wearing a light travel cloak with a decorative chain that was one of their big sellers. Dorothy and Affie had designed the cloak and the Frunge girl had engineered the chain.

"Any luck with the band?" Flazint asked.

"The equipment is here and they should be on their way. I hope a bunch of Horten girls show up because I sort of promised."

Flazint whipped out her tab and tapped away for a minute. "That should do it," she said, and showed the result to Dorothy. "Do you have any hats here or should I send a bot to our storeroom?" The Open Circuit listing had been modified to include, "Free hats to the first twenty Horten students."

"I probably have twenty," Dorothy said. "They stack well so they don't take up any room."

Affie arrived a few minutes later, accompanied by three Vergallian models, all of whom were wearing tube dresses from the SBJ Fashions "Basics" line. The three models made a beeline for the folding tables and begin eating fruit slices like they were starving. Dorothy would have sworn that one of the girls was crying.

"I used to work with them," Affie explained. "I promised we would get here before any press so they could eat something without getting fined. If we ever make the big time, I'd like to hire them away from the agency." She lowered her voice and added, "I was going to have them model the prototype gowns we've been working on for the ballroom line, but they're too skinny."

"What's with the lights?" Flazint asked. "It's like a classroom in here."

"I wanted to wait until the sound system and the food were set up," Dorothy replied. "My dad always controlled the lights so I was hoping to get Jeeves to do it, but he hasn't answered my ping. Let me ask Libby."

"Yes, Dorothy?"

"You were listening in just now, Libby?"

"With the ambassador gone, time weighs heavy," the Stryx librarian replied dryly. "You want to change the lighting?"

"Yes, please. We don't know how many people will show up, but I'd like to leave the area right around the ice harvester dark, the same with Dring's corner, and maybe just light a direct path from the corridor to the stage area where the band is setting up."

The overhead fixtures were either extinguished or dimmed, depending on their locations, and colored beams of light began playing over the area that Dorothy intended for the dance floor.

"You guys have a mirror ball?" Flazint asked in astonishment.

"All of the decks are equipped with emergency evacuation lighting that employs fine spectrum control, so we can adapt it to whatever biologicals are resident without changing elements all of the time," Libby explained. "It's good to give the circuits a workout every century or so."

"Where do we plug in?" a voice asked.

The girls turned and saw that a number of Hortens carrying instrument cases had arrived while they were watching the light show.

"Can you bring up the lights on the bandstand?" Dorothy subvoced, unsure how the musicians would feel about an omnipresent Stryx in the conversation. A white glow enveloped the small stage and the large mound of audio equipment.

"Cool," the Horten said, and started off with his bandmates before remembering something and turning back. "I'm Coffin, by the way. Death said he's stopping to pick up our food."

"Where's Mornich?" Dorothy asked.

Coffin checked to make sure that the other Hortens were out of earshot before answering her. "Death is Mornich. Our publicist came up with the stage names, and we aren't supposed to use our real names at a gig, even with each other."

"Got it, Coffin. Thanks for coming."

A sound like a foghorn came from the stage area when one of the band members began tuning his amplified trumpet, and as if somebody had thrown a switch, a crowd of hungry students and their friends materialized and descended on the catering tables.

"Did you guys get any models?" Affie asked the other two.

"The girls from my pledge circle will all be here with our accessories, but they may be a little late because they need to color coordinate their trellis work with the bags," Flazint explained. She turned her head as she spoke, and held up her handbag like the model in one of SBJ's corridor ads.

"The red works really well with your vines," Affie complimented the Frunge girl.

"Yeah," Dorothy said, biting back the comment that the color scheme reminded her of the holidays. "Oh, I better go and change myself. I'll wear our knock-off of my mom's old cocktail dress. I didn't call any models, but Chance said she'd wear our Number Eight."

"That's the one I rigged up with a platinum zipper," Flazint told Affie, as Dorothy disappeared into the dark.

"I still think we'd take over the whole market if you could engineer a silent version of that Velcro stuff," the Vergallian girl replied. Her face lit up when she saw her off-and-on boyfriend appear with a gang of Vergallian

166

friends in tow. "Stick! Over here. Why are you covered with dust?"

"The lift tube informed us that there was a traffic jam at the closest terminus to Mac's Bones and offered an alternative with a ten-minute walk across the corner of an ag deck," Stick said sourly. "Didn't tell us that pollination was going full tilt."

"I've never heard of a lift tube traffic jam," Flazint said nervously. "Do you think it's because of us?" She looked towards the entrance of Mac's Bones, and saw that the trickle of new arrivals had turned into a steady stream. Then she opened her handbag and pulled out her tab.

"What are you doing?" Affie asked.

"Removing our announcement from the Open Circuit," the Frunge girl replied. "I don't think that getting a crowd is going to be the problem."

Four hours later, the Gem caterers were on their third resupply run, despite doubling the amount of food they brought each time. The Horten band seemed determined to blow up the rental equipment, and there were well over two thousand young people from a dozen species jumping around the dance floor. The precision lighting scheme kept all of the partygoers packed together in front of the stage, and Dorothy found herself standing outside of Mac's Bones, taking a break from the volume of the sound.

"Bob Steelforth. Galactic Free Press," a reporter introduced himself.

"I know you, Bob, and you know me. I'm Dorothy, Ambassador McAllister's daughter."

"Sorry, you don't look like anybody's daughter in that dress," the reporter apologized awkwardly. "I heard there's a big cross-species flash event happening down here, and I'm covering the 'What's Up Union?' page for alignment weekend. I thought I'd drop in and file a real-time report, maybe get a feature out of it."

"Sponsored by SBJ Fashions," Dorothy said, her eyes lighting up. "That's 'S' as in 'Shaina', 'B' as in 'Brinda' and 'J' as in 'Jeeves.'"

"I see you've worked with the press before," Bob replied, filling in the details on his reporter's tab. "Can you tell me anything about how the party got started?"

"Well, my family is all gone for the weekend and I had the whole hold to myself, so I called a couple of friends."

"No prior advertising?"

"Just a notice in the Open Circuit."

"Any reason you didn't post to the Galactic Free Press events board for Union Station?" the reporter asked sharply.

"SBJ Fashions focuses on cross-species wear, so we didn't want a crowd that was mainly humans."

Bob acknowledged the truth of her reply with a grudging nod, and asked, "How long have you been in the business?"

"We started with a line of hats three years ago, and we've expanded into dresses and accessories. We outsource most of our manufacturing to the Chintoo orbital, but our bespoke line is hand-finished on the station. Ten percent of our profits go to the station shelter for underage labor contract runaways, and we're currently working towards a cross-species shoe that will revolutionize the market."

"Revolutionize the market," Bob repeated, as he finished entering Dorothy's statement. "Good luck with that. Mind if I go in and capture a few images?"

"Please, take lots. If you ping me afterwards, I'll identify any of our items for you."

"Great." The reporter stopped and opened the locket around his neck that many station residents wore for nose plugs to filter semi-breathable atmospheres. He removed a pair of plugs and stuck them in his ears. "Dual purpose," he told Dorothy. "Latest thing from the Dollnicks."

"Doesn't your ear wax clog the filters?"

"What?" the reporter shouted.

"Never mind."

Dorothy was about to follow Bob back into the party, when Chance showed up, dragging a reluctant-looking Thomas.

"I see my timing is as impeccable as usual," the fashionable artificial person said. "I'll cut up the floor with grumpy here and make sure that reporter gets a picture of me in old Number Eight."

"I'm really not comfortable with the idea of throwing a party in the EarthCent Intelligence training camp," Thomas protested.

"The only equipment we're using is rented, though Libby is manipulating the lights for us," Dorothy explained. "Don't worry. If my parents hadn't wanted a party in the hold, they would have put it in writing."

"Time to earn your keep, Dancer Boy," the artificial person said to her partner, and pulled him into Mac's Bones.

When Dorothy followed them back into the hold, it seemed like the band had become even louder, if that was possible. She fingered her own nose plug locket before grimacing and shaking her head. Dorothy kicked herself again for being unable to find her father's tool belt with its acoustic suppression field unit for working around noisy equipment. Suddenly, somebody poked her in the side, and the volume dropped off to the level of lift tube background music.

"Jeeves! Where have you been?"

"If I don't get in my multiverse hours every cycle, Libby gives me a hard time," the Stryx replied. "Good job drawing a crowd, but I see you charged the caterer's bills, a rush equipment rental, and a surprisingly expensive order of Horten take-out to the business account. Are we making any sales?"

"It's a flash event, we're creating good will. Affie and Flazint have friends modeling our products, and Chance says she'll get our dress on the front page of the Galactic Free Press," Dorothy said, exaggerating just a little. "It's not like we're taking orders tonight or anything."

"Did you run it past Shaina or Brinda?" Jeeves asked.

"They have families and lives, so I didn't want to bother them on a Friday night. It just sort of came together."

"You creative types," the Stryx said in mock despair. He floated alongside Dorothy to the refreshments table to inspect the catering that was blowing a hole in their marketing budget. Just as they approached, a girl in impossibly high heels stumbled and dumped a whole plate of cheese and crackers on the floor. An enormous paw shot out from under the table, covered the entire mess, and dragged it out of sight.

"I wondered where the dog was hiding," Dorothy said. "I'm surprised he can stand the music."

Behind the overhang of the disposable tablecloth, Beowulf finished scarfing down his latest haul, and then delicately reached with a paw for the Dollnick acoustic suppression field unit on Joe's tool belt. Long practice had enabled him to master extending just one claw, which he used to adjust the device up to its highest setting. He could still feel the floor vibrating from the heavy bass, but the only thing he could hear was his own breathing. Then he rolled back onto his stomach and brought his eyes up to the level of the slit he had made in the draped tablecloth.

# Fifteen

"You look like refugees," the president observed, on meeting the McAllisters in front of the door to EarthCent headquarters. He eyed their collection of luggage, puzzling over Samuel's cane, which was stuck through the straps of the boy's bag. "You're an hour early for our meeting. Did the hotel throw you out?"

"We're leaving later this afternoon, so it was either check out early, or go back to the hotel in the middle of the morning," Joe explained. "Room had to be vacated by 10:00 AM or they would have charged us a day at the full rate."

"I believe we might have made a mistake going with the lowest bid for the conference venue," the president admitted. "Oh well, there's always next time."

"I thought some of the sessions were pretty interesting," Kelly said. "And I'm glad Joe was able to take our son on some daytrips to see a little of life on Earth."

"I liked the Brooklyn Bridge," Samuel spoke up. "The guide told us all about working in caissons and getting the bends. Too much air pressure is like the opposite of working in space."

"I never thought of it that way," the president replied. "It's my favorite bridge too, though floaters are making all bridges obsolete. Now let's get out of the hallway and make ourselves comfortable while we wait for the others."

He stepped towards the door of EarthCent headquarters and attempted to swipe open the lock.

"So this is where it all happens," Joe said. "I'd sure like to get a look inside."

"Just two shakes of a lamb's tail," the president replied, misunderstanding the ambassador's husband. "We reprogrammed the locks after a, uh, incident, and the palm scanner seems to be thrown off because I've been carrying a hot coffee."

"I think he means the office next door, Stephen," Kelly hastened to explain. "Joe works closely with Thomas, an artificial person who has integrated a number of personality enhancements from QuickU."

"Try knocking," the president instructed Joe. "I'm afraid this lock just isn't going to work for me today so we'll have to enter through QuickU anyway. We share a lunch room."

"Will they be here this early?" Joe asked.

"They pretty much live there," the president replied. "You know geeks."

Joe knocked on the QuickU door. There was a thudding sound, and the door was opened by a young man with long hair who was seated in a wheeled office chair. After letting in the guests, the employee kicked off the wall and rolled back to his work station without saying a word.

"I often knock around this time," the president said, excusing his neighbor's lack of manners as he ushered the McAllisters into the office. "I'm not alone today, Carl. These people with me are friends of Thomas from Union Station."

Carl spun around in the chair, peered at the visitors through the shaded glasses that enhanced his holographic display, and then put his fingers in his mouth and gave a piercing whistle. Several more shaggy heads displaying various lengths of five o'clock shadow popped up from behind other workstations, and an attractive woman emerged from one of the few offices with a door.

"Good morning, Stephen," she addressed the president. "I take it from Carl's alert that you've brought us important guests." She surveyed the three McAllisters and paused on Kelly. "I know you. You're the auction ambassador."

"Kelly McAllister. This is my husband Joe and my son Samuel. We're sorry to disturb you so early in the morning, but my husband works with Thomas and…"

"THE Thomas?" the woman interrupted. "As in Thomas and Chance of Union Station? Of course, that's where the auction was. Then you're the Joe who Thomas works with training spies? This is an honor."

"Uh, thanks," Joe said, wondering what else the artificial person had told his QuickU friends. "Thomas always lets us know when he has a new personality enhancement on evaluation. You do really good work, well, except for the gambler one. Some of the regulars at our poker game are talking about banning Thomas until he agrees to stop using it."

"My fault," Carl said, raising his hand. "We didn't design the enhancement for social gambling. It's for making a career out of playing in casinos or insurance underwriting. He's already told us that he'll be deintegrating the gambler personality after he finishes testing it."

"You create artificial intelligence here?" Samuel asked.

"Oh, no," the woman replied, shaking her head at the very idea. "We deal strictly in enhancements. Think of it as packaged life experience with some algorithms to help the artificial people make sense of the data. I wouldn't know the first thing about creating viable AI."

"Don't the two go hand in hand?" Kelly asked.

"Sentience is a mystery to us," Carl said. "Everybody working at QuickU is fascinated by AI, but I don't think any of us are interested in playing god that way. Some of the aliens have it down to a science, but what I've seen of the human-created AI relies a great deal on luck and environment. They basically keep piling complications onto a rule-based system, give it mobility and sensory technology, and then throw challenges at it and hope that it develops consciousness in self-defense."

"So how do you create your enhancements?" Joe asked.

"The best ones are licensed from artificial people who have a strong skill set to offer, like the Dance Machine enhancement that Chance supplied and keeps up to date for us," Carl said. "If I was an artificial person, the first thing I would do with extra income is pay down my body mortgage, but Chance says that she spends all of the royalty money on clothes."

"You have a copy of Chance in a machine here?" Samuel asked, looking disturbed by the prospect.

"It's nothing like that," the woman reassured the boy. "Chance supplies us with a vector representation of the dance steps and moves that she's mastered, including those from over thirty alien species to date. Then, with the help of your Stryx librarian, she isolates and codifies an algorithm for fitting those movements to music and mood."

"I didn't know Libby was in the enhancements business," Kelly remarked.

"Any honest business is worth doing," Samuel declared, another mantra learned in Libby's school.

"I thought Thomas told me that his Secret Agent enhancement was compiled from characters in literature," Joe said.

"That was one of our early attempts," the woman explained. "The advantage is that the source material is license free because it falls under the 'transformative use' exclusion of copyright law. The disadvantage is that experiences gathered from fiction are, well, fictional, and then we have to synthesize the algorithm to process the data."

"I'm sorry, I don't think I ever got your name," Kelly said.

"Lucy Hui," the woman replied. "I'm the founder of QuickU, and thanks to night school, I'm now the legal counsel as well. These boys do all of the grunt work."

"I've had my own run-ins with contract law," Kelly said, accepting the founder's hand. "I'll never sign anything now without running it by our station librarian."

"Unfortunately, Earth doesn't have a resident Stryx," Lucy replied. "Still, our personality enhancements are all marketed as 'For entertainment use only,' so we're covered both ways." She glanced over the workstations that took up most of the floor space to a closed door with a red light above it. "Are you here to see Hep? He should be done with today's session in a few minutes."

The president, who had slipped away to open the front door of EarthCent headquarters from the inside, returned just in time to ask, "You have Hep in there?"

"He's volunteered to try to supply us with enough data points to create a Verlock mathematician enhancement," Carl explained. "Hep's mind is incredibly well organized, but he lacks an AI's interface options for data extraction."

"If you're successful, why would an artificial person want a personality upgrade to think like a Verlock mathematician?"

"It's sort of a public service thing for us," Lucy explained. "Hep is having trouble finding the right help for his reverse engineering project, and he's hoping that a free personality enhancement and good pay might attract some artificial people. Most of them have excellent innate computational ability, but working with theory is a completely different thing."

"Well, uh, don't drain him or anything," the president said. "We need Hep to run the project, and he's supposed to be meeting with a group of ambassadors in our offices in another forty minutes."

"We'll have him ready," Lucy promised. "Have your guests had their coffee yet? There should be a fresh pot in the break room, and I brought in three dozen donuts this morning, so you're welcome to whatever the boys haven't eaten."

"Coffee sounds good to me," Joe said.

"Thank you," Kelly and Samuel chorused.

The president led them into the lunch room that EarthCent headquarters shared with QuickU, and the McAllisters all stared in astonishment at the framed images on the walls. Half of them showed Thomas looking debonair in his Bond suit, or Chance mid-spin in her tango shoes and dress.

"I guess we're so used to seeing them that we forget how good-looking they are," Joe commented.

"Well, if you're going to take out a mortgage with the Stryx to pay for a body, there's not much point in going down-market," the president pointed out. "Grab yourselves a drink and a donut, but remember that we have catering coming for after Hep's presentation to the steering committee."

"If it's a spy thing and I can't be there, can I hang out at QuickU and see how they do stuff?" Samuel asked. "Maybe they'll make a copy of me for artificial boys."

"That's very noble of you, Samuel, but we actually invited the press to this briefing, so you're welcome to participate," Stephen responded.

"Is that wise?" Kelly asked, as she rifled through the donut boxes. "I thought the members of the steering committee were supposed to be confidential, and—come to Momma!" she concluded, uncovering a triple chocolate donut languishing alone in the third box.

"I take it you missed the Grenouthian documentary on human espionage through the ages that wrapped up with an analysis of EarthCent Intelligence, including an organizational chart with faces, names, and contact information," Stephen replied, but Kelly was lost in chocoholic heaven and didn't even nod in acknowledgement.

After the crumbs settled, the president led the McAllisters into EarthCent headquarters, which turned out to be an office suite not much larger than the embassy on Union Station. The hall led past two side-by-side doors with nameplates reading, "President Stephen Beyer," and "PR Director Hildy Greuen," and then ran into an open reception area about half the size of QuickU's shared workstation space. The receptionist's desk had been pushed over against a wall, and the room had been filled with rows of folding chairs, one of which had been moved to prop open the front door.

"I wasn't expecting much, but how can you run EarthCent out of this place?" Kelly asked in dismay.

"If I'm actually running anything, I'd like to know what it is," the president replied. "Besides, our offices are spread all over Earth, and we had over four hundred resident employees at last count. When EarthCent was first established, somebody thought that putting the headquarters in New York made sense, but that was before the Stryx announced the budget. Other than Hildy and the receptionist, the only other people working out of this office are our resident cultural attaché and a communications specialist. QuickU took over the lease years ago, and we actually sublet from them."

"Drat," Kelly said. "I was looking forward to confronting your human resources department about a few open issues."

"Luckily for them, they all work overseas," the president replied.

The front door pushed open, and Ambassador Zerakova entered with her husband and daughters, all toting their luggage. Joe went over to prop the chair back in the door after it shut itself, just in time to admit Ambassador White, who was wheeling a deceptively large carry-on behind her.

Over the next twenty minutes, the rest of the ambassadors on the intelligence steering committee trickled in, some with family members, all with luggage. The wall near the door began to resemble the unclaimed bags section of a spaceport. Leon arrived with his camera and tripod, and Samuel immediately offered to serve as his assistant again. The only other press to appear was a fourteen-year-old girl who presented credentials from the Lower East Side Student Journal. A minute before the meeting was scheduled to start, Hep wandered in from the

179

back hallway, and the president stepped up to introduce him.

"Before we begin, I'd just like to remind everybody that this meeting is attended by press, so let's try not to blurt out any secrets. Without further ado, our guest speaker is Hep, who is spearheading our project to restore the original Drazen jump ship under contract to their museum, I mean, Drazen Foods."

"It's not the original Drazen jump ship, it's the first one that worked," Hep corrected the president.

"Of course. So do you have a presentation you would like to give, or shall we just ask questions."

"Whichever is faster," Hep replied. "I really need to get back to work."

"Then we'll just go with the questions," the president continued unperturbed. "Could you start by explaining how jump technology works?"

"No," Hep replied bluntly.

"Is that because it would take too much time?"

"If I had twenty years to explain it wouldn't help," Hep said. "Don't you think if I understood how jump drives worked I would be creating my own design rather than attempting to reverse-engineer half-million-year-old Drazen technology?"

"But we've been assured by the Verlocks that you're the best human for the job," the president protested.

"I'm not in a position to argue with the Verlocks about anything, though I'd like to see their proof," Hep replied seriously. "I've been studying Verlock mathematics for most of my life, and I'm the only human to attain the degree of first rank mathematician."

"So you're as smart as any of them," the president said.

"First rank is the bottom, like the first rung on a ladder, or the first step on a journey."

"What about all the other humans in the Verlock academies?" Kelly asked.

"They haven't reached the first rung yet," Hep informed her. "Let me tell you a brief story. Last year I took my vacation from the project to return to Fyndal and my trip coincided with the visit of a Cayl scientist. The Verlocks were more excited than I'd ever seen them, and they declared a planetary holiday for their guest's lecture on multiverse mathematics, an area where the Cayl excel among the known biologicals."

"Did you make a recording?" Ambassador White asked eagerly. "It could prove the key to everything."

"I was able to follow the Cayl's derivation for exactly forty-three seconds," Hep replied sadly. "Verlocks all around me were getting up and leaving the lecture hall because they consider it rude to stay for a presentation which one doesn't understand. Since that's not a human tradition, I remained as the crowd thinned out. By the end of the presentation, the only two Verlocks remaining were the head of the academy, and young Fryklem, whose specialty is True Math."

"If a young Verlock was able to understand, it must be a question of inborn ability, of genius," Ambassador Fu observed.

"Fryklem is young for a Verlock mathematician, but he's well over three hundred in our years, and has been studying the whole time. I consider him a friend, so I didn't allow the normal rules of academic propriety to stop me from asking him to explain in dumbed-down terms what the Cayl had discussed. Fryklem told me that it was a proof for a mathematical transform that makes certain types of non-observable events computable, and that he expected it would keep him busy for the next five hundred years or so."

"What's this 'True Math' that you mentioned?" Kelly asked.

"At the risk of oversimplifying because my own understanding is defective, it's a complete reworking of the Verlock system that requires all solutions to be expressed utilizing a limited set of symbols that are believed to be valid everywhere, not just in our universe." Hep paused and let out a sigh, like a young man longing for an absent lover. "Think of it as a combination of mathematics and poetry, except the aesthetics are inaccessible to all but a few. It's nothing new to the Verlocks, but I'm told that only a handful of mathematicians in each generation are capable of contributing to the field and fully appreciating its beauty."

"So where do you see us in five hundred years?" the president asked. "Will our top people reach the level of the Drazens or the Hortens?"

"I can't predict the future, but I can tell you what we'll know five hundred, or even five million years from now," Hep replied. "Humans will discover the answers we are capable of comprehending to the questions we have the ability to conceive."

"Is that a riddle?" Ambassador White followed up.

"No," Hep said. "Anyone on Earth might look up and ask what happened if the moon suddenly went missing, but that's because we all know that it was there the night before. Our ability to ask questions, useful questions, depends on our current state of knowledge. In some ways, simply seeing what the advanced species are doing gives us a huge head start, but in other ways, it may hurt our development."

"What do you think about teacher bots?" the president asked. "Does having instant access to so much information improve a child's chance of growing up to be a creative and productive person?"

"Can I say something?" Leon spoke up. "My own experience with Stryx teacher bots is that they only respond to questions if humans have already figured out the answers. The lock screen on the bot always displays the message that its function is to help you teach yourself. It presents texts and problems, and it checks your progress by asking for solutions, but the corrections part is kind of limited."

"So if you make an error, the teacher bot doesn't always provide the solution," Kelly surmised.

"Not right away," Leon elaborated. "There isn't one right answer to lots of the stuff that we studied, but if you really can't figure out your mistake, you can put in a request for a more detailed solution and it usually shows up in a day or two. But the teacher bot always pushes you to try the community answer pool first, to see if another kid can explain it. That part is kind of fun."

"The teacher bots aren't true AI, but their programming often produces responses you might expect from a Stryx station librarian," Hep concurred. "The Stryx will decline to answer most questions involving advanced alien technology, in part because they want to see us develop organically, and in part because they see such knowledge as competitive information. The aliens, most of them anyway, are not hiding their basic math or sciences from us. The answers are in front of our faces, but we don't have the context to understand them."

# Sixteen

"How's Ballmageddon going?" Chastity asked her mother, hopping up to sit on the edge of Donna's display desk in the outer office of the EarthCent embassy. She twisted her neck in an attempt to read some of the hundreds of overlapping electronic notes displayed.

"I wish you and your sister would stop referring to the ultimate planning event of my life by that atrocious name," Donna replied irritably, clearing her display desk with a swipe. "Your ace reporter, Steelforth, has been in here twice a day pestering me with questions."

"Bob's a sweetheart, Mom. Besides, if he wrote anything about the ball that slipped by Walter and myself, you know that Libby handles our distribution over the Stryxnet. I'm sure she'd stop anything that could spoil the surprise. Wouldn't you, Libby?"

"Of course I would," the Stryx librarian replied. "But the information blackout is no longer necessary, as the ambassador and her family have left Earth and are on their way to boarding the Vergallian freighter for the trip home."

"That's what I've been waiting to hear," Donna said. "Please release the invitations for humans as soon as the freighter leaves Earth's orbit. Thanks to Kelly travelling direct rather than nonstop, there should be plenty of time for the president and the ambassador's family to attend if they feel like making the trip."

"Invitations queued and ready to go," Libby confirmed.

"Have you watched the Grenouthian documentary about balls yet?" Donna asked her daughter. "They've been running it three times a day."

"And I'll bet you're watching it three times a day," Chastity replied. "If you really want them to stop, knuckle under and send invitations to the bunnies who appeared in the production. That's obviously what they're after."

"Dring is in charge of the alien invitations, and he was already here telling me to do just that," Donna admitted. "He thinks the Grenouthians are doing Kelly a great honor by publicly pleading for a chance to attend. Sometimes I don't understand his logic. I suspect he's watching the documentary three times a day himself."

"I don't know where he'd find the time. Dring is meeting with every important alien functionary who accepted his invitation, and they started arriving two days ago to take advantage of the once-in-a-lifetime opportunity to speak with a Maker. Whenever he has an hour free, he's at our place taking tune-up lessons with Marcus or dancing with little Vivian. He's surprisingly light on his toes for a reptilian shape-shifter."

"Dragon sounds nicer," Donna reminded her blunt daughter. "Oh, I almost forgot why I asked you here. Daniel wants to see you."

"What about?"

"His conference, of course. What else does he care about this time of year? He said something about you suddenly having better sources of information on some of 'his' worlds than he does, and he gets regular updates from EarthCent Intelligence, as well as from conference members."

"Oh, we've been expanding our coverage," Chastity said casually. "Is he in now?"

"He's waiting for you."

The publisher of the Galactic Free Press approached Daniel's office, the door to which was open, and saw that the EarthCent consul was indeed waiting for her expectantly. The door slid closed after she entered.

"Hey, Chas."

"Hi, Daniel," she responded, taking the chair in front of his desk. "Was there something I could help you with?"

"I saw an interesting story in the paper this morning about a shortage of pizza toppings on Chianga."

"Do you have friends in the pizza toppings business?"

"Through my wife, though none of them sell dried Sheezle bugs."

"No, I don't imagine they would," Chastity replied cautiously.

"Then there was the story from Dolag Twelve about how the weather satellite grid was temporarily disabled by a massive solar flare and it rained for two days straight on the southern continent."

"That couldn't have been any fun for the human laborers," Chastity said. "The work on those Dollnick ag worlds doesn't wait on the weather."

"Oddly enough, the story didn't mention the crops or the work conditions at all. It focused on the cancellation of a soap box derby due to muddy road conditions."

The publisher of the Galactic Free Press shifted uncomfortably in her chair as she saw where Daniel was heading.

"My favorite story of the day is from a Drazen open world owned by the Two Mountains consortium," he continued. "It seems the miners broke into an ancient tunnel system with glassy smooth walls which may have been created by a long extinct species that vaporized rock in their mining process."

"That is interesting," Chastity said, and began to rise from her chair. "Well, if there's nothing else…"

"The focus of the correspondent was on the potential for using the tunnels as water slides," Daniel concluded.

The publisher of the Galactic Free Press sank back down into her seat, and there was a moment of awkward silence before she asked, "Libby? Does our contract allow me to talk to Daniel about this?"

"He's not currently on the list, but I'll add him," the station librarian replied.

"Does this make me a party to the contract?" Daniel inquired. "I promised Shaina not to sign any business deals without checking with her first."

"Just the nondisclosure agreement, unless you wish to decline," Libby replied.

"Fine, I accept. What's going on with the in-depth kiddy reporting?"

"Libby began experimenting with making the teacher bot infrastructure available for student newspapers many years ago," Chastity explained. "It grew out of the community answers functionality."

"What does Libby have to do with teacher bots?" Daniel asked.

"You didn't know that they're one of her projects?"

"I thought the Stryx just provided the basic programming and had them mass-manufactured on the Chintoo orbital."

"She does provide the basic programming, and the curriculum is modeled on her experimental school which your son just started attending. But so many human children have no access to real schools, and Libby wanted to provide a richer learning experience than they could get from a simple bot. Teacher bots that are close enough together form their own peer-to-peer network, and if the planet has a Stryxnet connection, it allows her access."

"In real-time?"

"Too expensive," Libby interjected. "Each bot network batches all of its daily communications for a single burst when the bandwidth is cheapest. If students have questions that need my attention, I reply the same way. I think the delay has actually proved beneficial since it gives the children a chance to work out the answers on their own or with other students."

Chastity shot Daniel a wry smile. "I thought InstaSitter was really something back when we first added the 'Over one billion sentients babysat,' to our ads, but Libby babysits over a billion students by herself."

"I guess I can see why you're keeping this secret for now," Daniel replied. "I can just imagine what the alien conspiracy nuts back on Earth would make of it. It must be an awful lot of extra work for you, Libby."

"It's a librarian thing," the Stryx replied modestly.

"So if you haven't guessed already, Daniel, I made a deal with the student newspapers to provide ad-free editions of the Galactic Free Press in return for the rights to republish some of their stories," Chastity said. "You probably noticed the change because you're so obsessed with your open worlds and we don't always have a lot of other news from those places, but it's really less than one percent of the content we publish."

"So when Mike comes home and tells me what he learned in school today, there are human children all over the tunnel network saying the same thing to their parents?"

"I customize lesson plans for each student in my school," Libby said. "If your son never shows an interest in math, I won't try to cram calculus down his throat. The limited time that any teacher has with students is best spent on helping them unlock their potential, rather than meeting some arbitrary curriculum."

"I know you have a lot of spare capacity for work, but can you really personalize lesson plans for a billion students?" Daniel asked.

"I don't even try," Libby admitted. "The data I get from the teacher bots isn't nearly as useful as what I learn about the children in my school through working with them directly and watching them grow up on the station. But the bots have access to an archive of over a thousand different paths to learning that I've developed over the years for students like your son. Of course every child is unique, but there's give-and-take in each interaction, and I believe most of the full-time teacher bot students are well served."

"Daniel? Can you come out here?" Donna's voice came over the office speakers. "We seem to have an issue."

Daniel rose from behind his desk and moved rapidly into the outer office, with Chastity right behind him. The entrance to the embassy looked like it had grown several metal arms and legs, and then he realized that there was an alien in a hard-shelled encounter suit stuck in the door.

"Hold up, stop struggling," Daniel said to the alien, hoping that it had the appropriate translation technology. The metal-encased feet on all four legs, or perhaps they were walking fins since the face inside the transparent bubble on the front of the suit appeared quite fish-like, halted their ceaseless scrabbling at the floor. "I can see over your, uh, shoulder, that you're wider in the corridor than you are in here, so moving forward isn't an option."

"Ball invitation," the alien requested curtly.

"The ball isn't really an EarthCent affair," Donna explained. "Dring, the Maker, is the one who is throwing the party and paying all the bills."

"Ball invitation," the alien demanded.

"If you leave your name, I promise we'll pass it along to Dring," Daniel offered.

"Ball invitation," the alien repeated a third time, its voice taking on a threatening edge.

Daniel ran out of patience with the rude creature and challenged it with, "Do you even know how to dance?"

To his surprise, the alien started to whistle a waltz, and its center pair of legs began lightly stepping through a dance figure, while it supported itself with its outer legs. The creature even held an imaginary partner in its arms, and inclined its head as if executing a dip, though being wedged in the door frame robbed the maneuver of any grace.

"How many do you need?" Donna asked in a resigned voice.

"Two," the alien responded immediately. "Myself and my brood partner."

"I guess we can make an exception this once," Donna said, hoping that Dring wouldn't count them against her allotment for humans. "To whom shall I send the invitations?"

"Supreme Dictator Vissss, temporarily residing at the Zifgit Hotel. Now, could you help me extricate myself?"

Daniel and Chastity stepped forward and pushed on the dictator's hard-shelled encounter suit, and with all four of his front legs scrabbling together, he suddenly sprang free like a cork coming out of a bottle. The back of his suit smashed into the corridor display panel opposite the embassy entrance, but neither seemed to be damaged.

Immediately after the jam was cleared, Lynx entered the embassy and asked, "What was that all about? I was stuck waiting in the corridor for five minutes. I tried knocking on the back of whatever that was, but it ignored me."

"Another ball aficionado," Donna replied. "Libby. Where does the Supreme Dictator Vissss hail from?"

"Vissss. It's the name of the volume of space administered by the Coryth in the Magellanic Clouds. We've never had a Coryth visit the station before, so I'm sure that Dring will be pleased."

"But how could the dictator have known about the ball, much less have arrived here in time to demand an invitation?" Daniel asked.

"I'm afraid I can't tell you that," the station librarian replied.

"Hey, I think we may have a different problem," Lynx said. "While I was waiting in the corridor, all of the display panels flipped to showing an ad for Astria's Academy of Dance."

"It's not surprising that the Vergallians would be looking to cash in on the ball," Donna said. "A week's worth of lessons could make the difference between causing a traffic accident on the dance floor and circling with your dignity intact."

"The ad wasn't for lessons. It read, 'Do you have a ticket to the EarthCent ball? Highest prices paid, discretion guaranteed. Contact AAD on the Vergallian dance deck.' I think the artwork of the couple dancing was ripped from the Grenouthian documentary."

"What ever happened to honor among aliens?" Donna complained.

"I lifted the local publication moratorium when the ambassador's shuttle launched," Libby informed her. "It's easy enough to prevent news about the ball from reaching Earth for the next few hours, and I'm sure that the crew of the Vergallian freighter will have the decency to keep it to themselves if they hear anything at their stopovers."

"Aliens are weird," Lynx muttered. "Didn't Dring give the Vergallians enough tickets?"

"He gave them the most invitations of any non-human species for the sake of aesthetics," Donna said. "A lot of the aliens aren't going to be able to handle the dances, and if we get many more looking like the Supreme Dictator Vissss, it will take all the upper caste Vergallians Dring invited to balance them out. Besides, I've been to enough competitions to watch Vivian and Samuel dance, and you have to admit that the Vergallians have style."

"Not to mention a dance deck," Daniel commented. "I never knew that, but I guess they're all fanatics and it must take up a lot of space. Why did the name of that advertiser sound so familiar?"

"Astria's Academy of Dance," Lynx repeated. "You've heard of it before because it's a well-known front for Vergallian Intelligence."

"They don't actually teach dancing?"

"Of course they do. It's the top dance academy franchise on the tunnel network, if not in this part of the galaxy. That's what makes it effective as a front."

"But what are they going to do with invitations for somebody else?" Daniel asked. "Isn't Gryph supplying station bots to confirm the identities of aliens at the door?"

192

"I thought that printing up souvenir tickets would be a nice plus for the humans," Donna admitted, taking an example out of her purse. "Dring insisted that the printer use real gold foil after I explained the idea. It wouldn't be easy for an upper caste female to pass as human, they just look too perfect. But I'm sure there will be a huge market for tickets with the Vergallian commoners, and all they really need to do is get a bad makeover."

"I'll bet that none of Kelly's friends sell their tickets," Daniel asserted.

"We're giving them awfully short notice, and some may have other commitments or be unable to make the trip," Donna pointed out. "I suppose there's no reason to worry about it. More Vergallians isn't going to hurt a ball."

"How about all of the aliens that Dring invited?" Lynx inquired. "Has Kelly even met any of them before?"

"I know that Dring got the Stryx to send a science ship to the Gem homeworld to pick up Gwendolyn, and he was trying to locate the retired high priest of Kasil, but most of the guests are just important leaders from species that Dring has come across in his travels. I thought he was doing it all to honor Kelly, but he told me that when he made the list, he realized that he couldn't invite some of the high-whatnots and not the others without putting them at risk of a war."

"Hey, everybody," Shaina said, entering the embassy with her daughter in a baby sling. "Mind if I hang out here? Brinda warned me that our old friends from the Shuk were showing up at SBJ Fashions to beg for tickets, and I figure it's just a matter of time before they try me at home."

"We just caved in and promised invitations to an alien dictator, and I imagine it won't be long before everybody thinks of trying the embassy," Daniel said. "Maybe we should all just go into hiding for the rest of the week."

"It's better to face them down now so we don't create the expectation that we'll give in," Donna said philosophically.

"May I suggest blaming Dring for the ticket distribution?" Libby chimed in. "He won't mind, and everybody outside of your immediate circle of friends is too awed by him to protest."

"Works for me," Daniel said immediately. "I've got another holo-conference scheduled in—two minutes ago, so I have to get back to work. You and the little chipmunk are always welcome," he added, addressing his wife and the baby. Then he retreated into his office and closed the door.

"I liked him better before he began taking his job so seriously," Shaina said. "I guess I'll head into the office and tell Brinda the company line on invitations."

"Hold on a second," Donna requested. "I've been watching your son on Aisha's show and it's the first time I've ever seen subtitles. It seems they only pop up when Mike is speaking to the Drazen boy."

"I'm always in the studio when they shoot so I haven't seen them myself, but I'll bet it's the first time they've had a child speaking, or trying to speak, an alien language," Shaina explained. "I guess the Grenouthian engineers are afraid that Mike's Drazen isn't good enough for all of the Drazen children watching, but they don't want their translation technology dubbing over it in real time since he's trying so hard."

"I never would have noticed," the office manager replied. "I guess my implant doesn't have any trouble making sense of what he's saying, so I thought he was just speaking English."

"That's probably because he gets the words right but his syntax is more English than Drazen," Lynx speculated, having participated in her share of language training sessions in the EarthCent Intelligence camp. "That's pretty cool that he's speaking an alien language on the show, and the Drazens must take it as a compliment. How's that little Stryx from Libby's school that Mike and Fenna pal around with working out?"

"Spinner?" Shaina paused and smiled. "He's settling down, and he really brings a fresh perspective to the broadcast. Even though he knows so many facts, I'll bet that if you took a vote, the audience would say that either the little Horten girl or the Verlock child is the smartest kid on the show. On the first day, they all thought that the little Stryx knew everything."

"Which language does Spinner speak?" Lynx followed up.

"English. He can translate from any language into any other language if you ask him, but he's only comfortable expressing himself in English. What do the Stryx think of Spinner's performances, Libby?"

"I think he's the best bit of public relations we've had since Gryph and the other first generation Stryx saved the galaxy from the killer AI."

"What do the other Stryx think?" Donna inquired.

"None of them admit to watching, aside from Jeeves, and you know him. He wants to stand in for Aisha if she ever takes a vacation."

# Seventeen

"That must be it," Kelly said, pointing out of the shuttle's window at a ship with Vergallian markings docked at the transportation hub. "It looks much bigger than the one we came out on."

"That donut section is a centrifuge for the living quarters," Joe commented, looking out his own port from the seat behind his wife's. "Hopefully they'll spin it up once we're underway."

"Why wouldn't they?" Kelly asked.

"Some of those freighter captains know how to squeeze a cred until it cries for help. Maybe they'll tell us that there's an extra charge if we want to feel gravity, or worse, they could run it fast if they're adapted to a heavier world, and then charge us to lighten up. You never know with the Vergallians, they occupy so many planets."

"It's a 0.91 G ring," Samuel asserted, looking out at the ship. "The rating is painted on the hull."

"There you have it," Kelly said. "It looks like we're in for a pleasant trip home. I don't know about you two, but I'm looking forward to a week of being out of touch with everybody. Sometimes I feel like all of this communications technology just doesn't give us time to catch our breath."

"It's a good thing they don't spin the transportation hub, or we'd have to hire a porter to help with our luggage," Joe commented.

"I know I brought too much, but for what we're paying, it didn't make sense to let the personal baggage allowance go to waste," Kelly replied defensively.

"I didn't mean your clothes and stuff, Kel. I was thinking about that giant cooler of fresh fruit that Glunk sent. Samuel and I had enough trouble just loading it into the shuttle, and we'll never eat it all before it spoils."

"Vergallians like some of our fruit, especially citrus," Samuel said.

"Make sure you get something in trade," his father told him. "The aliens will think less of both you and the fruit if you don't put any value on it."

"I, for one, will be glad for the change from those dehydrated meals we brought for the trip out," Kelly added. "I know that you're going to say that they were gourmet compared to the field rations you used to live on."

"It's just that I already ordered all of our supplies for the return trip from the chandler's on the hub. Don't tell me what the overweight charges were for this shuttle. Mass equals fuel to get off a planet, but taking the space elevator instead would have added another day to our trip."

"I negotiated with the ticket agent while you were loading the cooler," Kelly said proudly. "I think he was new, because he let me bill the charges to EarthCent."

"Hope he doesn't lose his job over it," Joe replied.

An hour later, the McAllisters left the chandler's shop and began shuffling along the concourse of the transportation hub on their magnetic cleats. Joe and Samuel strained against the momentum of their loosely bundled baggage as they turned into the docking arm that led to the Vergallian freighter. Ahead of them, a body stretched and contorted, trying to make contact with one of the surfaces of the docking arm, but somehow the unfortunate individual had ended up floating in the very center of the tube.

"Hang in there, Miss," Joe called out. "We'll be there in a second."

"If you throw something you'll move in the opposite direction," Samuel added helpfully.

Her slow rotation finally brought the woman's head around to face the McAllisters, albeit upside down, and Kelly recognized Hannah, the young woman from her conference session who had dreamed of being kidnapped by an alien.

"Ambassador McAllister," the girl cried when she recognized her rescuers. "I can't believe it's you. I took your advice to travel on a freighter and this was the cheapest ticket to Union Station I could find."

"My wife didn't mention magnet cleats?" Joe asked.

"I can't think of everything," Kelly replied. She pushed her carry-on at Joe, who resignedly undid one of the bungee cords that were threaded through the handles of the other bags and food containers that he and Samuel were already shepherding, and added Kelly's. In the meantime, the ambassador grabbed the upside-down woman's shoulder, reached high above her own head to get a hand on Hannah's knee, and spun her gently around.

"I can't thank you enough," Hannah gushed, "I was starting to feel sick from being upside-down."

"It's all the same in Zero G," Samuel pointed out. "If you've never been before, it takes a while to get used to."

"So how are we going to work this, Joe?" Kelly asked, still holding onto the girl who wore a full-sized backpack.

"She can ride on the cooler and the three of us can handle the mass together, at least until we get on the ship. How did you get this far, Miss?

"One of the passengers from the space elevator offered to tow me along to the docking arm since his departure gate was past here. He gave me a push down the center but I sort of drifted to one side, if a tube can have a side. When I made contact I was facing the wrong way, and my pack hit one of the ribs and got stuck. Struggling made things worse, and somehow when the pack worked free, I was barely moving."

"If you went through all of that without throwing up, you'll do fine in space," Joe told her. "Hold on to the cord and don't be surprised if I grab your foot when we get there. It's easy to start things moving slowly in Zero G, but it's rare that you have the same time to slow down. Your mass will just stretch that bungee cord out like a rubber band if we need to stop or make a hard turn."

"Did you send anything ahead, or is that pack all you brought?" Kelly inquired of the young woman, as the group resumed its shuffling journey towards the Vergallian freighter.

"It's everything I own," Hannah said. "I don't plan on returning to Earth, and I wouldn't have enough money for a ticket anyway. I sold all of my apartment stuff, but some of it was only mine on credit, and I had to pay off the bank before the space elevator agency would sell me a ticket."

"All of your clothes and food for the trip are in that one pack?" Kelly asked doubtfully.

"I'm an expert backpacker. I used to go hiking with one or two other girls in the mountains every chance we got, because..." she hesitated, glancing at Samuel and Joe, and then whispered, "You know."

"Are those sorts of, uh, encounters we talked about at the conference supposed to take place more often in the mountains?" Kelly guessed.

"The aliens can't just land in cities and kidnap women. Everybody would see them."

"Grabbing your foot now," Joe warned the girl, as they reached the open airlock of the freighter. The three upright people and the unified clump of baggage with Hannah holding on fit easily through the hatch, which was intended for both crew and miscellaneous cargo. They cycled through, and when the inner doors slid open, they were met by a middle-aged Vergallian man with a purser's tab.

"Nice of all my passengers to show up at the same time," the purser said in a friendly voice.

"What did he say?" Hannah asked Kelly.

"You don't have an implant?"

The young woman shook her head in the negative. Kelly explained to the girl that while the crew members likely had implants that would allow them to understand English, none of them would speak it.

"She doesn't have an implant and she's never been in space before," Samuel told the purser in Vergallian.

The purser blinked, threw the mental switch on his own implant, and demanded of the teen, "Say that again."

Samuel repeated himself, and the Vergallian broke into a wide smile. "I've met a few humans over the years who could get by in our language, but you speak like a royal consort. Let me show you all to your quarters and then I'll introduce you to the crew. Can I give you a hand with all this stuff?"

Joe accepted the help gladly and winked at his son. He knew that Samuel's fluency in Vergallian had made all of the difference in the way the crew of the Earth-bound ship had treated them, and he was pleased to see that it was looking the same for the journey back.

The purser led them through a series of long passages, which were thankfully large enough to accommodate the makeshift load of luggage, with Hannah riding on what she perceived as the top. After almost five minutes of shuffling along on their magnetic cleats, they arrived at a door with a graphic image of a humanoid figure being decapitated after sticking its head through an opening.

"Centrifuge ring," the Vergallian announced. "We're primarily a container carrier, and the engines and jump drive are in their own section at the end of the central keel, so there's no reason to access the cargo section once we're underway. Most of it is open to vacuum in any case."

"You mean that once the ring is up to speed, there's no way to get from the living quarters to the rest of the ship?" Joe asked. "How about the engineering crew?"

"If there's an emergency, they take a lifeboat, but our chief engineer is fond of saying that repairs are for ship-yards. Most of these container carriers run everything from an operations room in the centrifuge ring, and the engineer can always remote into the maintenance bots."

"Sounds like you don't need a very big crew."

"Just fourteen of us, plus five spouses and twelve kids. We all inherited our shares in the ship. My own family invested before the keel was laid."

"How long ago was that?" Kelly asked.

"I'm twenty-fifth generation, so around two thousand years," the purser estimated. "She's practically new."

"How can a ship last so long, Joe?"

"No rust in space," her husband reminded her. "All of the alien ships use active shielding to protect against dust and debris, so barring an attack or real careless handling, the structure is good until metal fatigue from stress and radiation sets in. The engines are bolt-in replacements."

"The Vergallians have battleships that are over a million years old," Samuel told her enthusiastically. "Some of them take thousands of years to build."

"Don't they use bots?" his mother asked.

"To build warships? That's like, sacrilege," the boy replied.

Kelly decided to drop the conversation, using the excuse of translating Samuel's half for Hannah, since her son had persisted in speaking Vergallian.

"Deck is always blue," the purser told them as they entered the stationary ring through what would later become the ceiling, and then shuffled down the curved wall to the deck. "It's not like we can spin up in a hurry, but it's always a good idea in Zero G to know which way will be down when we get going."

The four humans were soon settled into their cabins, which were surprisingly roomy for a freighter. When Kelly asked the purser about the capacity of the ring, he explained that they often carried livestock between colony worlds, and most of the animals couldn't tolerate Zero G for long, even when heavily sedated. After that, she regarded every old stain on the bulkheads with suspicion.

As soon as they detached from the transportation hub the donut began to spin up, and the constantly changing angular acceleration slowly pressed them against the outer surface of the ring, which now became the deck. Following the purser's advice, they all tried to take a nap for the tunnel transit away from Earth. After they woke and had a family breakfast, Kelly took some fruit and went to check on Hannah.

"Thank you so much," the young woman said, accepting the gift. "I only packed dried fruit because of the weight."

"What are you making there?" the ambassador asked.

"It's a dress I was working on that I couldn't leave behind," Hannah said, holding up the unfinished garment. "The sweatshop where I worked let us come in on Sundays and rent the sewing machines for personal use. I couldn't finish this one in time to sell it, so I'm redoing it for myself. It's been a while since I did a seam this long by hand," she added ruefully.

"You worked in fashion? That's my daughter's business."

"Oh, I'd so love to meet her, maybe she'll hire me. I wouldn't say that I worked in fashion, though. The sweatshop was just the best job I could find with my lack of education, and it was all piecework, so I'm pretty fast."

"I'm sure Dorothy will be happy to meet you. You can stay with us until you get settled in," Kelly added impulsively.

"I couldn't," Hannah protested, but it took no great effort for the ambassador to talk her into it, after which they went together to explore the ring that would be their home for the next week.

Cries of encouragement and applause led them to what must have been the main social room, where an area was set aside for holographic projections. A popular Vergallian drama from the previous season was being shown, and a few of the crew's complement had moved into the hologram to play their favorite characters. The power of the projection was calibrated so that the participating crew members remained visible, and to Kelly's surprise, Samuel had taken the role of a sword-wielding guardsman. In place of a real sword, he flourished his grandfather's cane.

"If you love me, don't let them take me," cried the star of the drama, an impossibly beautiful upper caste actress who managed to convey the mixed emotions of over-whelming fear with the haughty disbelief that anyone could disrespect her person.

"Rally to me," Samuel shouted in Vergallian. He lunged at one of the oncoming holographic swordsmen with his cane, taking the attacker through the chest. The boy's uncanny mimicry of the voice and his fluid movement in the envelope of the character he was playing brought another round of applause from the watching crewmembers.

The action built to a crescendo, with Samuel parrying a rain of blows and shouting encouragement to the few guardsmen who had remained loyal. Then the hologram suddenly winked out, leaving a fourteen-year-old boy with a cane and a few middle-aged Vergallians clutching imaginary sword hilts in empty hands.

"Sorry, everybody," the purser announced. "The license on the copies I bought for this trip doesn't allow binge-watching. The next episode will have to wait a standard day."

"You were great," a ten-year-old Vergallian girl complimented Samuel. "You must have seen this drama like a million times."

"Maybe twice, but I practice with a fencing bot that can do scenes from immersives if you preload them."

"You what?" Kelly squawked, interrupting the conversation.

"Hi, Mom. I was just telling her how I practice fencing with the bot that Herl gave the training camp."

"Since when are you interested in fighting? The only reason I ever agreed to let you start dancing three hours a day was because I thought it would encourage your artistic side."

"It's dueling, not fighting, Mom. It is art."

"You were very good, even though I couldn't understand what you were saying," Hannah told him, drawing a scowl from Kelly.

"You can tell he's trained in dance from his footwork," the friendly purser contributed. "We have open ballroom practice every evening, though I don't know how your clock lines up with our day."

"I'll be there," Samuel promised. "We're all going to get jump-lagged anyway, so we may as well live on your clock while we're here."

"Does your father know about this sword practice business?" Kelly demanded.

The boy shrugged indifferently. "I don't know why you're so mad. It's not like I'm going to join the mercenaries or anything."

"So why are you studying dueling."

"A gentleman must learn the three D's," Samuel replied with dignity. "Dancing, dueling and diction. Diction is the hardest."

The emergency lights blinked on and off, which was the signal for entering or leaving normal space. In this case, they were emerging from the Stryx tunnel at Forcroft, one of the later planets to be added to the Empire of a Hundred Worlds.

"Ugh," Hannah said, moving a hand to her belly and then to her head. "What was that?"

"We just exited the tunnel," Joe informed her, having tracked them down. "The feeling of dislocation is proportional to the distance traveled outside of normal space divided by the duration, so the Stryx intentionally lengthen the time in the tunnel for biologicals to lessen the effect. When ships jump with their own drives, they also stretch the time as much as practical, but it takes extra energy, so there's the cost to consider."

"We can't be at Union Station already. They said that the trip would take over a week!"

"We're at the first stop," the ambassador explained. "It's a direct flight."

"That's so cool," the girl said, brightening up considerably. "I assumed it was nonstop, but this way I'll get to see a little more of the galaxy."

"We probably won't be allowed to leave the ship," Kelly told her.

"That's right," the purser said, showing that he had been following their conversation. "We aren't even docking at any of the stops. We just release the magnetic couplings on the appropriate containers for each destination and they get picked up by the local shipping contractors. Tugs will match our speed and bring us any outgoing containers as we position for the next jump. It's all off network from here until Union Station."

"How can you swap cargoes in just a few hours?" Samuel asked.

"That's the load master's job," the Vergallian explained. "He always knows where the containers we take on are heading, so he piles them onto the keel in an order that allows us to release the drops without doing any rearranging. But ninety-nine percent of this cargo is pig iron from the Sotti asteroid belt destined for the Chintoo orbital. The stops in between pay for themselves and maintain our status in the shipping guild, but their main purpose is to break up the jumps."

"Could we visit your control room for a jump?" Hannah asked. "I've never seen one before."

"You feel them more than you see them, but you're welcome to come and watch," the friendly purser replied. Samuel translated for the young woman, and she smiled happily. There were lots of jump descriptions in the alien romance novels she had been addicted to, and she wanted to see how much they got right.

# Eighteen

"This will be our only meeting before the ball," Donna informed her ad hoc committee. The gathering took place in the patio area of the ice harvester in Mac's Bones, and included all of Kelly's friends, who had been stunned to receive invitations to a major event just one week before it took place. "Does anybody have any last-minute questions or recommendations?"

"What are we going to do about drinks for some of the aliens we've never encountered before?" Ian inquired. "Between the Empire Convention Center's catering staff and the Little Apple merchants, I'm sure we have eating covered, but I wasn't convinced that the Dollnick running the Empire's cash-bar knew what he was talking about."

"He promised me that they could synthesize a reasonable facsimile of a beverage for all of the aliens I've invited," Dring reassured the restaurateur.

"Synthesize," Ian huffed. "That's what I'm worried about."

"It's a minor detail, and it will only affect the aliens who humans may never encounter again," Donna said, putting a practical spin on the matter. "How are you doing with the names, Woojin?"

"I'm sorry, Donna, but even with Libby's coaching I find most of them impossible to pronounce. I can manage the Vergallians and Drazens without a problem, but I thought we would only have time to announce the heads of empires. Other than the Cayl, I'd be lucky to get any of those names out without biting my tongue off."

"Ahem," Jeeves said.

"Alright, you've been my fallback position all along," Donna told the Stryx. "The entry will be down the grand staircase, so we'll have to get all of the alien dignitaries lined up in the lobby or they'll never make it inside before the dancing begins."

"Will I be introducing the McAllisters, or will they arrive before the various heads of state?" Jeeves inquired.

Donna paused and chewed her lower lip. "I haven't figured that out. Dring?"

"If the ambassador is in the ballroom with all of the invited guests before the dignitaries are announced, that would mean the surprise is already sprung," the Maker observed. "Perhaps the best thing would be to complete all of the introductions and only bring Kelly and Joe to the ballroom afterwards."

"But how will we maintain the secret between the time the McAllisters arrive home and the time to leave for the ball?" Donna asked. "Is there something you can do, Libby?"

"I'll cheat their implant times and alter the deck lighting so they'll think it's almost midnight when they return," the station librarian replied. "I'll also edit Kelly's news feed just in case she checks, but after all of the off-network stops that freighter is making, they'll be so jump-lagged that they'll want to go to sleep according to the clocks just to get back on schedule."

"That would be great," Dorothy enthused. "I've already made her ball gown and arranged to rent a tux for Dad. I'll wake them up an hour before the ball and tell them that it's a birthday party for Dring being thrown by the Stryx. There's no way Mom would miss that."

"How about that decorative watch that Kelly wears?" Lynx asked.

"I'll take care of it," Jeeves offered. "Remote reprogramming is a specialty of mine."

"Where do we stand on the news coverage for the ball itself?" Donna asked, turning to her younger daughter.

"I've been in almost constant contact with the Grenouthians ever since Dring released the additional invitations for their high mucky-mucks, who practically begged for tickets in the documentary about balls," Chastity replied. "They wanted press passes for so many immersive camera operators that it would have been wall-to-wall bunnies in there, but when I put my foot down, they backed off immediately and offered to use autonomous floating cameras. They're bringing in their top hosts from the news channels to interview the important aliens, but I made them promise to stay off the dance floor."

"It sounds like they're excited," Clive remarked.

"I've never seen the Grenouthians so worked up before," Chastity replied. "They're so flustered by the concept of a human being at the center of the greatest multi-species social event in ages that sometimes they even forget to be condescending. If the bunnies didn't know that it's all thanks to Dring, I think they'd be having nervous breakdowns."

"How about Galactic Free Press reporters?" Donna asked.

"We're sending all of the full-time Union Station correspondents and editors to maximize our opportunity to cultivate alien contacts. The live ball coverage will be a pictorial stream with Walter and I doing the captions. Of

210

course, we'll try to get interviews as well, and we can publish full transcripts of any speeches in the back section."

"Have you finished lining up all of the speakers for the Hall of Praises, Dring?" Donna asked.

The Maker's shoulders slumped, and his large eyes took on a tragic expression. "Despite my best efforts, none of the leaders from species who haven't previously encountered humans were willing to go on the record praising Kelly. Emperor Brynt was the only guest who was enthusiastic about the idea, and I'm afraid that the other empire-building species consider the Cayl to be eccentric."

"Given the news coverage and the chance to appear on stage before such an important audience, I'm sure that all of the local ambassadors would be willing to speak on short notice," Daniel suggested.

Dring shook his head. "I miscalculated by inviting the leaders of so many off-network species. You know I'm not one to stand on formalities myself, but if I've learned one thing about diplomacy through my long life, it's that power structures must be respected. Other than Emperor Brynt, none of the other potential speakers have the standing to address the likes of Dictator Vissss or Horde Leader Gantu. Imagine if a Grenouthian broadcast showed one of them looking away and yawning while a tunnel network ambassador was speaking."

"So what are you saying, Dring?" Donna asked.

"The Hall of Praises is not to be," the Maker replied. "I'm sorry to introduce a change in plans at the last minute, but I believe if we use the space as a card room for non-dancers, everyone will be happier."

Donna hid her relief that Dring was conceding defeat on organizing an evening of speeches and hurried to cement the alternative before he could change his mind.

"Clive. Can you figure out what card games all of the aliens play, and make sure that we have the decks or whatever else is needed?"

"Not a problem," the director of EarthCent Intelligence responded. "My question for you is, have you heard back from any of the so-called 'Fives' I asked you to invite? It would be nice if we could help sort out this Vergallian mess before somebody gets hurt."

"All but one accepted," Donna replied. "I only remember her because she has more A's in her name than any upper caste Vergallian I've ever encountered. Aarania."

"Too bad," Clive said. "According to our analysts, out of the names we dug up she's the best candidate for being in charge of the movement. Of course, it could turn out that our sources are all wet and that we've wasted a dozen invitations on members of a legitimate historical preservation society."

"It would be a feather in the ambassador's cap if we could deliver a diplomatic coup at the ball," Dring said, perking up noticeably.

"Alright, then," Donna declared. "You're all welcome to come to the orchestral rehearsal tonight, though it will probably be a madhouse. I sent invitations for the rehearsal to every person who ever attended one of my monthly mixers, and even with the short notice, the place will be packed. And thank you again for reserving the extra night and providing refreshments, Dring."

"Thank Gryph," the Maker replied.

As Beowulf mooched scraps and people began heading home, Jeeves materialized at Dorothy's side and said, "I've asked Shaina and Brinda to stay for an emergency SBJ Fashions meeting."

"Emergency?" Dorothy repeated, trying to buy time. She had a sinking feeling that she knew what this was about. "I'll try pinging Flazint and Affie, but I think they may both be on night time."

"I already woke them and they're on their way," Jeeves replied with none of his usual flippancy. "Perhaps we can move inside for privacy."

"Alright," she said nervously, leading the way up the ramp into the ice harvester.

Shaina and Brinda sent their husbands home with the children, and Dorothy suddenly felt like the youngest person in the room. There was some awkward conversation until Flazint and Affie arrived, the former looking a little wilted and the latter like a beauty queen. Jeeves launched into his subject matter without any introduction.

"Seven thousand creds for a party when you include the cleaning bill, and that's rounding down," the Stryx complained. "Please explain to me what we got in return."

"I think we earned a lot of goodwill with influencers from all of the species who attended," Dorothy replied, not bothering to pretend that she didn't know what he was talking about. "And Chance did appear on the front page of the Galactic Free Press wearing one of our dresses. The reporter even got the initials right in our company name."

"Death earned a lot of goodwill with influencers by stripping off his clothes while he was singing," Jeeves retorted. "I've been monitoring the social traffic for all of the station species since your flash party, and if you do the math and adjust for the statistical norm, which I did, each additional mention of SBJ Fashions cost us three hundred and twelve creds."

"But that's more than my weekly salary," Flazint exclaimed.

Dorothy shot her friend a look and tried to defend the strategy. "Goodwill can't be quantified that easily, it takes a while to seep in. Chastity always talks about the need for repeated exposure to get results from ads in the Galactic Free Press."

"Thank you for reminding me about the paper," Jeeves responded. "While it's true that Chance appeared on the front page wearing one of our dresses, that was strictly the Union Station edition. Do you think that people around the rest of the galaxy are interested in reading about university parties taking place so far away that they'll all be long dead before the light reflecting off the station can reach them? And speaking of readers, how would you describe the human demographic we're targeting?"

"You know," Dorothy said, though it wasn't something she had ever bothered putting much thought into. "Young women, mainly. Teens, twenties, early thirties?"

"Really?" Shaina drawled. "You think I'm too old to wear our clothes?"

"That's not the point here," Jeeves continued, as if he were prosecuting a trial. "Teens, twenties, and early thirties. You couldn't have done a better job describing the demographic least likely to read the paper."

"David reads it every day. He pays for an ad-free subscription," Dorothy protested.

"And your boyfriend is in the habit of buying women's clothing and accessories?"

Dorothy clamped her mouth shut since she couldn't think of anything else to say. It had been quite a lot of money to blow on a party.

"Jeeves isn't angry with you, girls," Brinda said in the silence that followed. "It's just that he feels—we feel," she amended herself, making a gesture that included her sister, "that the three of you haven't adjusted to the realities of running a business."

"Do you remember what our profits were last cycle?" Shaina asked the young designers.

"About six hundred creds," Affie replied.

"That's our office rent," Flazint corrected her.

"It was positive, right?" Dorothy asked.

"It was nine creds," Shaina told her. "On almost a million creds in sales, we netted nine creds. After three years in business, we really hoped to be much further along."

"And next cycle it will be a loss," Brinda added.

"Of around seven thousand creds," Jeeves grumbled.

"Do we need to raise our prices?" Flazint asked.

"Finally," Jeeves said. "A suggestion that doesn't involve an expensive new prototype, followed by production setup costs, only to be told that you've come up with something better before the first delivery even reaches the station. Sometimes I think you're all doing it on purpose to make me look bad in front of the other Stryx."

"We didn't know," Affie argued. "You didn't explain it. I've never been in business before."

"So here's your chance to learn," Brinda said. "From now on, we want you to create a business case for introducing new products. Shaina and I are both convinced that the current cross-species lineup is gaining traction with residents on the stations where we have a presence, but we're cutting our own throats with so many new product introductions."

"But designing new clothes is the fun part," Dorothy protested.

215

"And making a profit is the work part," Jeeves retorted. "I don't want to be labeled the mean Stryx who takes away the punch bowl when the party gets started, but in retail, past performance is a highly reliable indicator of future failures."

"So no more flash fashion events?" Affie ventured.

"Short of providing free samples to twenty million InstaSitters, I can't think of a faster way to throw away money."

"Jeeves! You're a genius," Dorothy cried.

"You do have a gift for stating the obvious, but why just now?" the Stryx responded.

"It's the perfect way to reach young women on stations all over the tunnel network without spending a dime on marketing," the girl continued enthusiastically.

"Aren't you forgetting something?" Shaina asked.

"Well, some of them are males, I guess, but even the younger girls will have money to spend because they're earning it babysitting."

"Do you think you could talk InstaSitter into it?" Affie asked.

"InstaSitter is Blythe, Chastity and Tinka. I'm friends with all of them."

"Aren't you forgetting something else?" Shaina tried again.

"Well, giving samples to all of the InstaSitters could be overexposure," Dorothy replied. "Maybe Tinka could help us pick a smaller group, like girls who have worked a certain number of assignments, or who have been with InstaSitter a long time."

"You're forgetting the cost of the product," Jeeves thundered, unable to keep it bottled up any longer. "Whether it's two million or twenty million, who is going to pay to manufacture all of these promotional gifts?"

"Oh. Well, the business side is your job. We just come up with the ideas," Dorothy responded brightly. "Maybe Libby will loan you the money."

"To give away," Jeeves pointed out. "Then instead of one foolish Stryx on Union Station, there will be two."

"It would come back to us ten-fold!" the girl enthused. "I thought you said you liked doing all that marketing math. This could be our big break."

"You want me to do the math? Fine. Let's say we give away lightweight travel cloaks to just one percent of InstaSitters. Thanks to somebody's insistence on using a metal clasp rather than synthetic material," Jeeves paused and dipped in Flazint's direction, "the manufacturing cost is six creds. Figure one percent of InstaSitters comes to around two hundred and ten thousand, so your giveaway, assuming InstaSitter handles the distribution, will cost us over twelve hundred thousand creds."

"That's less than a million," Dorothy said hopefully.

"No, it's one point two million," Shaina corrected her.

"But I've seen our travel cloaks selling for twenty-four creds in boutiques," Affie pointed out. "Even if it takes four giveaways to sell one cloak, we'll break even."

"No," Brinda said. "If it takes four giveaways to sell one cloak, we'll lose six hundred thousand creds, because we sell them to the boutiques for twelve. And you should understand that it's only the Stryx infrastructure that allows us to ship direct from Chintoo to stores, eliminating middlemen. If you ever do business away from the stations, you'll find out that wholesalers and distributors take a large cut, not to mention all the extra shipping costs."

"How many giveaways will it take to sell one cloak?" Dorothy demanded of Jeeves.

"It's impossible to answer with precision because I don't have any close comparisons to work off of," the Stryx hedged. "It's true that InstaSitters enjoy a certain cachet on the stations, and a travel cloak which might be worn every day over other garments could maximize exposure. Predicting the potential behavior of over two hundred thousand young females from so many different species involves a large number of calculations, and then I have to estimate how the various sentients who see an InstaSitter wearing our cloak will react…"

"Stop delaying, Jeeves," Dorothy cut him off impatiently.

"One and a half," the Stryx admitted.

"Does that mean we'll make a profit?" Affie asked.

Shaina made a restraining gesture with both hands to quiet the younger women who sat to either side of her and addressed Jeeves. "Are you sure you're taking all of the factors into account?"

"It seems a bit unbelievable, but our branding on the cloak is prominent, and it's always worn as the outer layer. I wouldn't recommend marketing lingerie this way."

"I came up with a good business idea," Dorothy crowed. "Does that mean I get a raise?"

"Actually, I believe it was my idea," Jeeves reminded her. "You were simply the first to acknowledge my genius. Does anybody want to hear the conversation played back?"

"I think both of you may want to delay taking credit until the actual sales results are in," Brinda said. "You're really, really sure about this, Jeeves? Can you check your math with Gryph or something?"

"It's a one-off," the Stryx explained. "After the first giveaway, the effectiveness will diminish to the point of negative returns, but I took the novelty into account while doing my calculations. And I fudged increased sales of our other products into that one-and-a-half number—the cloaks will just about break even. Most of the profits will be due to the InstaSitters who receive a freebie purchasing something else from us."

"So we're not fired or anything?" Flazint asked.

"I can't fire you," Jeeves told the Frunge girl. "It was in the terms of the first loan I took from—the Thark said what?" he interrupted himself. There was a loud "pop" and the Stryx vanished.

"Did our boss just run away from our meeting?" Affie asked.

"He's not responding to pings," Dorothy replied.

"Jeeves only goes supersonic when he's in a real hurry," Brinda told them. "I'll bet he's off the station by now."

"Libby? What happened to Jeeves?"

"A prior business commitment," the station librarian responded. "Don't worry. I'm sure everything will work out fine."

# Nineteen

A piercing alarm siren began to wail, and a hard lurch caused Kelly to miss the piece of bread with the butter knife, thus spreading a liberal serving of raspberry preserves on her arm. The streak looked more blue than red under the emergency lighting.

"What's happening, Joe?" she demanded, looking around to make sure that Samuel hadn't been thrown into a bulkhead.

"I'm guessing it's either a general power failure or we've been hit with some kind of energy suppression field, though it will take quite a while for the ring to spin down."

"I'm going to the common room to ask," Samuel announced, and fled before his parents could object.

"Does this sort of thing happen often on space trips?" Hannah asked nervously.

"It's not unheard of," Joe reassured her, and rose from his bolted-down chair to go after the boy.

"Wait, we'll come with you," Kelly said, and failing to locate the napkins, licked the jam off her forearm. "Ready."

The three adults followed in the boy's footsteps to the common room, where most of the crew had gathered around a holographic projection. It showed a close-up of a warship, with a swarm of little figures in bulbous orange spacesuits heading directly towards the camera.

A young Vergallian woman entered immediately after the humans and breathlessly reported, "The captain sent me to say that all communications are being jammed. The vessel that halted us is positively identified as the imperial class destroyer that went missing from the home fleet several weeks ago. They've disrupted our power and are demanding that we turn over our passengers. The captain said to prepare to repel boarders."

"Hold on," Joe shouted, trying to draw the attention of the Vergallians, who began retrieving weapons from the lockers lining the bulkhead of the common room. He had to grab the purser to get the crewman to listen. "You can't fight marines in armored spacesuits. Just one of those guys could carve up this ship with his suit weaponry."

"Vergallians don't submit to acts of piracy, even if the criminals are from our own navy," the purser replied curtly.

"Tell them something they'll listen to, Samuel," his mother urged. "We can't let all of these people get killed just to protect their honor."

"We'll have to go to the bridge and talk directly with the captain," the boy said decisively. "Follow me."

Again the adults found themselves chasing Samuel through the central corridor of the centrifugal ring, and they entered the control room that served as a bridge for the freighter just a few seconds behind him.

"Do not sacrifice your families in a meaningless gesture," a beautiful woman on the main display was saying as they came in. "You have my word of honor that your passengers will not be harmed."

"That doesn't give you the right to stop and board a free Vergallian merchant vessel," the freighter's captain replied in an icy tone. "I think you'll find that we're worth our salt."

"Invite us!" Samuel shouted at the screen image in Vergallian. The freighter captain spun about in irritation at the interruption, but the upper caste female on the screen immediately shifted her gaze to the humans.

"I, Aarania, extend a cordial invitation to our human friends to spend one day aboard my ship, after which I will personally see that you are re-embarked on transport direct to Union Station."

"We accept," Samuel declared formally, waving off the freighter captain's pleas. "We await arrival of a craft suitable to the transfer of my mother, the EarthCent Ambassador, and her luggage."

"Agreed," Aarania said, and the display image shifted to the outside, where the figures in combat suits were executing U-turns with varying degrees of grace.

"Bunch of amateurs," the freighter captain grumbled. "I would have shown them a thing or two."

"We appreciate everything you've done for us, Captain," Kelly said diplomatically. "You have my sincere apology for causing a delay in your schedule."

"What's happening?" the purser demanded, pounding onto the bridge in an exoskeleton suit that bristled with weaponry.

"It seems that the boy has denied us our chance at glory," the captain replied in a wondering voice, as if still coming to grips with the rapid change of fortune.

"Those of us with children on board thank you," the purser told Samuel. "We are a lightly-armed container vessel, after all, and such a mismatch can only end one way."

"Looks like she's sending the captain's gig," another of the crew commented, as a large craft emerged from a hangar bay in the destroyer's side.

"How will they dock with the ring?" Joe asked the purser. "It doesn't feel like we've lost any rotational speed with the power outage."

"Without power we're riding on mechanical roller bearings, and barring further interference, the ring takes days to spin down without rocket braking. I imagine the pirates will match our angular acceleration and extend a temporary airlock. That's well within the capability of any naval craft."

"Let's get our bags and meet them," Joe said to Hannah and his family. "I think it would be best for everybody if none of the destroyer's crew set foot on this ship."

After they gathered their belongings, Samuel spent the remaining time assuring the crew that his parents felt deeply honored by their willingness to sacrifice themselves. A short distance away, Kelly was working equally hard to lower Hannah's expectations.

"I can't believe this is actually happening," the young woman repeated for the third time in a row. "Do you think they'll let me choose who takes me?"

"They aren't kidnapping us," Kelly told her, marveling at how quickly the whole alien lover business had reasserted itself in her new friend's imagination. "Aarania promised that we'll be on our way in twenty-four hours, and the upper-caste Vergallians would rather die than break their word."

"If you say so," Hannah replied, but she sounded a bit skeptical. If Kelly had to bet on which possible outcome the girl would prefer, her money was on a handsome Vergallian pirate.

The captain's gig proved to be a utilitarian craft manned by extremely polite Vergallian marines, and the transfer went smoothly. Once aboard the destroyer, a friendly sailor even provided Hannah with a pair of magnetic cleats, after which the humans were immediately escorted to the bridge.

"I am Aarania," the perfect Vergallian woman in charge introduced herself, though she made no attempt to approach the humans. Then she turned to one of the bridge crew and ordered, "Commence communications blackout. I want no spurious radiation from the ship until this is over. Terminate the power suppression field and execute jump."

The two events must have taken place almost simultaneously, because Kelly just glimpsed the running lights on the Vergallian freighter that filled the display screen coming back on at full strength, before the unsettling feeling of a faster-than-light jump hit her stomach. The screen came back on faster than she expected, and the captain said, "Again."

This time, the queasy feeling was even more pronounced, and Kelly had the urge to sit down on the deck. Joe put a comforting arm around her waist to support her, and murmured, "She's taking evasive maneuvers to prevent tracking."

"Again," the captain said as soon as they reentered normal space, and the third jump lasted about the same amount of time as the second.

"You can't hide from the Stryx," Samuel blurted in Vergallian.

Joe winced at his son's choice of conversation starter. The accent was perfect, but the message was confrontational, and probably the last thing some renegade

Vergallians wanted to hear. To his surprise, Aarania favored his son with a brilliant smile.

"Not for any amount of time, I'm sure. But our analysis of Stryx interference in the naval affairs of other species indicates that three random jumps are enough to keep them guessing for a while. Again," she ordered as soon the ship reentered normal space. "And that makes four."

"But you swore you would only hold us for one day," Kelly protested when she recovered her balance.

"I will keep my word. I also respect the resourcefulness of your son in helping me defuse an embarrassing stand-off, and I wanted to demonstrate to him the futility of hoping for an equally dramatic rescue during your stay. Where did you get the idea of asking for an invitation, young sir?"

"Scions of the Empire," Samuel replied, naming an old Vergallian drama series. "I watched all of the episodes last year."

Aarania nodded solemnly. "Then I suppose it's too much to ask you to keep out of trouble." She raised her eyes and addressed the tallest of the marines escorting the humans. "Take them to their quarters and see that they have everything they need."

"What do you gain by holding onto us for just twenty-four hours?" Kelly asked, as the others turned to leave the bridge.

"That, Madame Ambassador, is a military secret," Aarania responded.

Joe spent most of the walk to the drop shaft explaining the fine points of shuffling along in magnetic cleats to Hannah, who was just beginning to get a feel for it when the sensation of weight began to return.

"Are we accelerating?" Kelly asked Joe.

"I'd guess only in the spinning sense," he replied. "These military ships fight in Zero G, but they can spin on their own axis to create varying degrees of weight, not unlike Union Station. Many species require it for health reasons."

Their escort brought them to one large cabin, the state of which gave the impression that the former inhabitants had vacated in a hurry. On the plus side, it had its own bathroom, and there was even an entertainment system, which Samuel found immediately. Unfortunately, it had been disabled.

"You heard Aarania," said the member of the bridge crew detailed to remain inside their cabin door to keep an eye on the humans. "Communications blackout includes entertainment systems."

"How about my toy robot?" Samuel asked, drawing his prized possession from his bag and setting it on the floor. The robot's eyes glowed green, it threw the guard a salute, and then a few sparks leapt from its casing.

"It's interfering with the interior suppression field," the officer shouted, and drawing a weapon, fired on the little robot. There was a blinding flash, and then the toy seemed to sag in on itself, as if something had melted.

"What the hell are you doing firing so close to my wife and son?" Joe yelled, and stepped aggressively towards the officer. The Vergallian thumbed a switch on his weapon and fired at the ambassador's husband, who dropped to his knees as if he had been caught by a hard uppercut to the jaw. While he tried to shake it off, Samuel pulled his grandfather's cane from the straps of his bag and leapt forward.

"En garde," he shouted in Vergallian.

The officer showed his quick reflexes by grabbing the end of the cane with his free hand and yanking it towards him to pull the boy off balance. His poise failed when he found himself holding a hollow wooden sheath and confronted with a long, thin blade.

"That's for stunning my Dad," Samuel cried, sticking the point into the officer's shooting hand. The Vergallian dropped his weapon and grabbed reflexively at the wound, only to find the tip of Samuel's sword-cane had moved to his throat.

The door slid open, and the marine on the threshold halted in his tracks as he assessed the unexpected situation. He noted the two women struggling to help Joe regain his feet, glanced at the smoking robot, and shook his head in disgust at the officer. After preventing his companion from entering, the marine dragged the officer's dropped weapon to the door with his foot and picked it up.

"Inform Aarania," he instructed the marine who remained outside. "I'm staying here to make sure this glory hound doesn't get lucky and cause more problems."

"It was their fault," Samuel's captive said weakly. "The boy deployed some kind of robot."

"Just shut up and try not to cut your own throat on his sword," the marine barked. He shook his head and addressed the humans in an apologetic tone. "Nepotism. He's a cousin of Aarania's."

Joe, who was just beginning to shake the cobwebs from his brain, nodded in sympathy with the professional soldier. A few minutes later, his head had cleared and he started rubbing his knees, thankful that his weight was at most a quarter of its usual measure. If it had happened under normal gravity, he doubted his sixty-year-old kneecaps would have survived.

Aarania showed up a moment later, made her own silent assessment of the situation, and addressed Samuel's captive. "Congratulations, Cousin. You've been taken hostage by an underage Human. Well done."

"Get him to put down the sword," the captive pleaded.

"As long as he's guarding you, you've effectively removed him from combat. It appears you are good for something after all."

"But you declared a communications blackout and he activated that toy robot. I think it was trying to send a distress signal."

Aarania leaned around the marine and peered at the remains of Samuel's Libbyland toy. She frowned. Then the lights blinked out, and there was total silence for a second before the emergency battery back-up took over with a clunk of mechanical relays. The beautiful Vergallian spoke into her personal comm but received no response. Then a perfectly circular section of the bulkhead vaporized, and Jeeves appeared in the opening.

"Next time, I suggest housing your guests on an outer deck to save damage," Jeeves said, floating through the hole. "On the bright side, the emergency atmosphere retention field that covered my hull breach seems to be holding, but you might want to have your crew throw up a patch after I leave."

"Stryx!" Aarania hissed. "So this is how you practice noninterference."

"Please move out of the way," Jeeves said politely. "I have no intention of interfering with your affairs, but I find myself trapped by the rapid response clause included in the warranty for my young friend's robot. I've gotten much more conservative about extending warranties since then, but it was my first."

"What are you talking about, Jeeves?" Kelly squawked. "You're just going to leave us here?"

"I don't think the Thark who I hitched a ride with in return for providing your precise location will go along with that. Now everybody please cover your eyes while I carry out this repair. It involves high heat."

A white glow began forming around the Stryx's pincer, and the biologicals all reflexively squinted their eyes shut. There was a click, a scraping sound, and a hollow clank, after which Jeeves announced, "All done."

Even Samuel looked away from his captive to stare at the restored robot. It gleamed like the day he had brought it home from Libbyland, and its eyes were glowing a healthy green.

"You didn't repair anything," Aarania's cousin protested, feeling his courage coming back as the sword moved away from his throat. "You just swapped it for a new one that you had in your casing."

"All within the terms of the warranty, I assure you," Jeeves replied. He projected a hologram of dense text that must have run into tens of thousands of words, if not more. "You can read it if you want."

The regular lights came back on, and Aarania stood stiffly for a moment as she digested a flood of communications from her officers. "If you would all be so kind as to accompany me to the bridge," she said in a defeated voice, and then stalked out of the cabin.

"I'm fine," Joe insisted, shaking off Kelly's arm and limping after the Vergallians, who had given up any pretense of holding the humans captive in the presence of the Stryx. Samuel retrieved the wooden sheath of his cane and carefully reinserted the blade before following.

"It's at least twice the size of our largest attack carrier," an officer was saying as the group entered the bridge. It wasn't possible to judge the dimensions of the enormous vessel displayed on the view screen without another ship for comparison, but it conveyed such an impression of power that everybody was willing to take the officer's calculations at face value.

"What are their demands?" Aarania inquired.

"Her commander told us to bring the Humans to where he could see them, and then he closed the channel."

"It's a Thark battleship. I recognize the class from historical records, but I thought they'd all been scrapped millions of years ago. What's the name on her prow?"

"Loss Prevention."

"Join me within the white line," Aarania instructed the humans, who shuffled forward on their magnetic cleats. The image on the main display instantly changed to the face of an angry Thark, blown up to ten times its natural size.

"Deliver the ambassador and her party immediately and I will leave your ship intact," the Thark said bluntly. "You're going to need a navigable warship if you wish to survive this debacle, and I would advise against returning to Vergallian space any time in the near future. For your sake, I hope you can transfer four-hundred thousand creds to the off-world betting parlor on Union Station to cover our expenses."

Aarania blanched, but she nodded her assent. The destroyer's crew members were too well versed in the pecking order of the galaxy to even suggest fighting a Thark battleship, no matter how old it was.

The McAllisters and Hannah gathered their luggage and transferred with Jeeves to the Thark ship, which jumped the moment they entered the airlock. A robot met them after they cycled through and escorted them to the bridge, which was manned by a handful of Tharks in casual dress.

"You appear to be whole," the Thark captain said, looking Kelly up and down. "Do you feel well?"

"Yes, thank you," the ambassador replied, surprised by the Thark's solicitude. "I'm glad to see that my embassy manager once again ignored my explicit instructions and bought us travel insurance."

"Travel insurance?" The Thark burst into rasping laughter, and his clan brothers followed suit. "Travel insurance covers a maximum of five thousand creds, including claims for lost baggage and emotional trauma. I wouldn't get out of bed to prevent a travel insurance claim."

"Then why are you here?" Kelly asked. "Jeeves? Did you put the Tharks up to rescuing us?"

"I wish we were here doing the Stryx a favor," the Thark captain growled on being reminded of the cause for his mission. "My idiot uncle made the biggest underwriting miscalculation of the century, probably because he was licking soap. Who grants fifty million creds of key person insurance on the ambassador of a new species without even checking on her travel arrangements? The premium didn't come anywhere near covering the charge for taking the Loss Prevention out of Union Station's long term parking, though the station's owner did make us a deal."

"What's key person insurance?" Kelly asked.

The Thark regarded her with sympathy. "It means you're important, but before you ask, I can't tell you why. I do request that you ping your embassy manager the moment we return to the station and tell her that the

Tharks will appreciate anything she can do for us. She'll know what I mean."

"Are we going to Union Station now?" Hannah asked.

"Including a taxi to take you into Union Station's core, you'll be there within a few minutes of your originally scheduled arrival time," the Thark replied. "We are taking the jump as slowly as our schedule allows since the distance in real space is appreciable. Please make yourselves comfortable, and don't touch anything that looks like a weapons control system."

Woojin met them at the arrivals area on Union Station and thanked Joe heartily for bringing along the heavy canister. "Looks like you might be on the disabled list for a few days," he added, observing Joe's limp.

"Getting stunned is like falling off a bike. You never forget how. Feel up to a beer before bed?"

"No thanks, Joe. Busy day for me to—, uh, tomorrow. We'll see you then."

Dorothy, Paul, and Aisha were all waiting up in the ice harvester, but they professed exhaustion when Kelly attempted to tell them the story of the kidnapping and rescue. Samuel said goodnight, and disappeared into his room with his little robot and his sword-cane, before his mother could think of confiscating it. After a few minutes of contagious yawning, Beowulf watched in approval as Joe, Kelly, and their new houseguest headed off to bed at ten in the morning. Then he stretched out for a mid-morning nap of his own.

# Twenty

Dorothy led the family through the Empire Convention Center, piling on more and more imaginary details about Dring's supposed birthday party to keep her mother from guessing what was going on.

"He's way older than a hundred million, and we couldn't find enough candles for the cake on Union Station, so we just spelled it out with chocolate."

"I thought you said the frosting was chocolate," Kelly objected. She was a little fuzzy after sleeping for ten hours, but she hadn't protested as Dorothy helped her into the most elaborate dress she had ever worn. "How would anybody be able to read it?"

"David used white chocolate for the numbers," her daughter fibbed, steering them towards the entrance to the main ballroom. "Did I mention that he baked the cake himself?"

"Isn't this the entrance to the main ballroom?" Kelly asked, coming to a halt. "Why is there a curtain?"

"To keep the heat in," Dorothy improvised, leading them into the antechamber. "Dring is always a bit cold, you know, so the curtain at the top of the stairs keeps all the warm air from getting sucked out the doors. Here, stand with Dad at the front."

Kelly turned her head to look suspiciously at her daughter as the curtain was drawn open, so she missed seeing the thousands of formally dressed ball-goers from over a hundred species shouting, "Surprise!" Then the McAllisters were covered in a shower of confetti, and Jeeves, wearing a silk sash that proclaimed him the Master of Ceremonies, floated up the broad staircase to welcome them. The Stryx turned to face the crowd, and despite her genuine shock, Kelly noticed that the back of the sash carried an ad for SBJ Fashions.

"EarthCent Ambassador Kelly McAllister and family," Jeeves announced in a thundering voice. The guests all exploded in cheers again, and Jeeves spoke to the surprised couple directly over their implants, saying, "What are you waiting for? Walk down the stairs so the orchestra can start playing."

"I'm going to kill Donna," Kelly yelled in Joe's ear. The orchestra struck up a waltz, and the guests rapidly withdrew towards the edges of the enormous room. "It's Ballmageddon!"

"Dring," Joe addressed the Maker, who stood beaming a toothy dinosaur smile at the foot of the stairs. "I banged up my knee yesterday and I don't want to spoil the first dance. Can you take her?"

"With pleasure," Dring responded, formally bowing to Kelly and extending a hand with blunt talons.

The ambassador was still numb from the surprise, but she took the proffered appendage and followed Dorothy's hissed instruction to curtsey, before letting Dring lead her out onto the empty dance floor.

Bob Steelforth, who had placed himself next to Brynt since the Cayl emperor was the most important guest he knew and could hope to interview, asked the bear-like alien, "What do you imagine they're saying to each other?"

Brynt concentrated on the waltzing couple for a moment, his furry ears twisting on his head for directional gain, and then informed the reporter, "Dring is repeating, 'One-Two-Three,' over and over again. Wait, Kelly just asked why nobody else is dancing. That's my cue."

The Cayl straightened up and stalked directly across the room to where Empress Pava was waiting, and then he whirled her out onto the floor. Soon after they were joined by Dictator Vissss and his brood mate, Horde Leader Gantu and his posse, and then the floodgates opened to mere royalty and diplomats who crowded onto the floor.

"She's not that great," Jonah told his sister, as they watched Ailia float by with Samuel. "Come on, I'll dance with you."

"Did you see her cheekbones?" Vivian asked miserably, ignoring her brother's hand. "I'll bet if you checked with a laser protractor they'd be within a hundredth of a degree of the parallel with Samuel's. They move like they're one person."

"She's two years older than you, and those Vergallian royals have the best dance coaches in the galaxy," Jonah said. "Besides, it's not like she can give up her rule and move back to Union Station."

Vivian sighed sadly, but the music was doing its work, so she accepted her twin's hand, and the twelve-year-olds glided out onto the dance floor.

"Come on, already," Dorothy said, tugging on David's hand. "You promised."

"As soon as they play something I know," the young man replied. "This isn't the one you practiced with me."

"It's a waltz," Dorothy insisted. "You can sit out later if they do dances where you need to know the steps."

"One beer," David pleaded. "There has to be a bar around here somewhere."

"May I have this dance?" a cultured voice inquired from behind Dorothy's shoulder.

"Metoo!" she cried. "Where have you been? I haven't seen you in ages."

"Do you like my suit?" the young Stryx inquired, floating back a step to show off the black pants he had belted around the lower part of his metallic casing, so the cuffs barely touched the floor. The jacket sleeve didn't quite fit right around his pincer, but Metoo had never been a clothes horse.

"Yes, and I'd love to dance with you," Dorothy said, placing one arm on his casing and taking his pincer in her other hand. As Metoo waltzed her out onto the dance floor, the girl turned her head and stuck out her tongue at her boyfriend.

"I can't believe everybody managed to keep the secret," Blythe admitted to Herl, as the head of Drazen Intelligence expertly threaded them through the traffic on the dance floor.

"I was worried about the humans, but I never doubted the advanced species, if you'll forgive the expression," Herl replied. "I almost feel sorry for Aarania and her 'Fives' movement. She must have sensed that it was now or never to take such a risk, but I would have given ninety-nine to one odds that her plan would backfire, even without the rescue. Out of all the species in the galaxy, the Vergallians are the last ones who could justify interfering with a ball for any reason."

After Joe lost sight of Kelly and Dring in the mass of dancers, he began limping his way around the edge of the dance floor to the card room that Jeeves had told him about. He was surprised to encounter Donna and Stanley watching the action from the sidelines.

"What's your excuse, Stan?" he asked his friend. "I thought dancing at a ball was your wife's dream."

"Putting on a ball, not dancing," Stanley replied. "Look at her, she's in a daze. I'll bet she can't even hear us. Of course, she hasn't slept more than a couple of hours a night for the last week."

"Well, I'm going to try to get a seat at a poker table," Joe said. "I haven't lifted a card in a month." Two limping steps away from the Doogals, he found his path blocked by a giant beetle.

"You are Joe McAllister," the Farling stated. "The station librarian requested my presence at the ball to handle medical emergencies. I can fix that knee for you if you'd like."

Joe glanced around to see if anybody he knew was listening before replying, "I think I'll just give it another day to see if it improves on its own."

"I understand," the Farling replied. "Good luck with the cards."

There was a crash from the dance floor as two aliens in metal-reinforced environmental suits collided, and the giant insect scuttled off to see if his services were required.

Near the entry to the card room, Joe encountered a heavily scarred Vergallian woman, standing alone with her back to the bulkhead.

"I guessed you were here when I saw Ailia dancing with Samuel," Joe said. "It's amazing how well they move together after not even seeing each other for eight years."

"They practice every day," the former Fleet captain and current Royal Protector replied. "I worried that she was spending so much time alone, and as her older half-sister, I thought I had the obligation to find out what was going on. She's uses a Stryx device disguised as a toy robot that provides real-time holographic communications. The technological prowess of the AI is humbling."

"So that's how Jeeves knew where we were and guided our rescue. Did you hear that the Tharks underwrote my wife's appearance tonight?"

"I have no doubt that immersive studios around the galaxy are rushing to produce bad dramas depicting the whole affair," Baylit said, smiling with the side of her face that wasn't a mass of scar tissue. "You are living proof of the expression Vergallian children use to describe the only acceptable excuse for having ignored chores and home-work."

"What's that?"

"Saved by the ball."

Joe snorted, invited Baylit to dinner at Mac's Bones the next evening, then he entered the card room and found an open seat at a poker table.

After several waltzes, the orchestra began playing a modern composition, and Donna hurried across the room to talk with the conductor. A dozen Tharks linked their arms and began doing a line dance, but everybody else took a break and began quaffing the refreshments offered by the Empire Convention Center catering staff.

"Twins," Chastity said, approaching Lynx and pointing at the cultural attaché's wrist.

Lynx almost fainted on the spot. "What?" she croaked. She resolved to kill both her husband and that Farling quack if Chastity knew something that she didn't.

"Twins," Chastity repeated, holding up her own wrist and displaying the black countdown watch. "I'm at thirty-seven weeks, two hours and eleven minutes."

"You got help from the Farling doctor too?" Lynx asked.

"One of our new reporters thought that he could land an interview with a visiting alien dignitary by sticking his foot in the door, but the door didn't agree. I took him for treatment, and the med bay has scanners that check everybody who enters. The beetle told me that I'm pregnant, gave me the countdown watch, and said I should quit eating pizza with garlic when it comes time to nurse. How about you?"

"Forty weeks, three hours, eleven minutes and eight, seven, six seconds," Lynx replied, checking her watch.

"What are you two talking about?' Kelly asked, approaching the pair while fanning her face with one hand.

"We're both expecting, and the Farling doctor who recently set up shop on Union Station passes out these delivery countdown watches as gifts," Chastity explained.

"It must be the doctor's idea of humor," Kelly said with a laugh. "Nobody could predict a time of birth that accurately."

"He only guarantees it within a twenty-four hour window, but he said if I keep to a strict diet and work schedule, that would increase the accuracy," Lynx explained. "Our payment is held in escrow until my black-haired, brown-eyed son arrives. The Farling said he couldn't put a precise number on height since a lot depends on nutrition. He offered me twins for a thirty percent surcharge, but I wasn't ready for that."

"Well, he seems like a very caring doctor."

"Not in our sense of the word, though I guess he was pretty nice for a giant bug who looks down on humans."

"And you trusted him for this?"

"Libby vouched for his work. It's just that Farlings don't care for humanoids in general. They refer to humans as Vergallian Lite."

"Like a diet product?" Kelly had never spoken with a Farling herself, and was beginning to have trouble following the flow of the conversation.

"He didn't have a lot of experience with humans, but he said we're basically Vergallians with some of the good parts taken out. Then he said that he's cross-bred dogs from different worlds that have more genetic space between them than humans and Vergallians."

"He's really good with allergies," Chastity added. "It used to be that Marcus couldn't eat peanuts without going into shock, but one visit to the Farling and he's cured."

"What was the treatment?" Kelly asked.

"He said we weren't smart enough to understand his explanation so he wasn't going to waste his time trying. Marcus drank something the Farling gave him and that was it."

"Here you are, Ambassador," Dring said, handing Kelly the glass of champagne he had gallantly offered to procure when they left the dance floor. "I hope you ladies are enjoying yourselves."

"Very much, though ironically, Marcus is so tired from giving last minute dance lessons that he's dead on his feet." Chastity said. "He's supposed to be getting us drinks, but my guess is he's sitting down somewhere."

"Champagne for all," Walter proclaimed, approaching the group with a tray of pre-poured glasses that he had lifted from one of the many strategically placed tables around the periphery of the room. He was accompanied by Brinda, Shaina, and Daniel, all of whom welcomed the break from dancing.

"It's a wonderful evening, Dring," Shaina addressed the Maker. "What made you think of a ball?"

"Donna told me that it's been Kelly's secret ambition to have one ever since she arrived on Union Station," Dring explained. "Do our humble efforts meet your expectations, Kelly?"

"The ball exceeds my wildest dreams in every way," the ambassador replied. "I'm looking forward to paying Donna back at the first opportunity."

--------------------------------

The orchestra quit when their contracted three hours was up, but Thomas bribed a half a dozen musicians who professed knowledge of tango music to continue playing after Jeeves announced that dinner was served in the main exhibition hall. Joe limped out of the card room to escort Kelly in to dinner, and neither of them was surprised to see that Samuel and Ailia ignored the change of program and continued dancing around the room to the music in their own heads.

"How's Vivian taking the return of the prodigal Vergallian?" Joe asked his wife.

"Better than you might expect," Kelly replied. "Blythe told me that she explained to the girl about Vergallians maturing so much slower than humans and that Ailia will likely be forced to make a political marriage to preserve her family's domain. I think Vivian's strategy is to wait and see. She's only twelve, after all."

"I'd add ten to that for being Blythe's daughter." Joe rubbed his stomach. "You wouldn't believe how hungry I am. I wonder what the hold-up is," he added, as they came up against the backs of a crowd of aliens.

A large, leathery figure loomed up beside them. "Follow me," Srythlan boomed, and moved off at his top speed, which left Joe thinking they would have been better served waiting in the slow-moving line. The Verlock ambassador led them out of the ballroom, and then through a side entrance into the large hall, which was now filled with hundreds of round tables. "We are at the head table," he explained ponderously as they approached the dais at the front of the room.

Most of the guests had indeed found their seats while the slow-footed Srythlan was taking the McAllisters on his shortcut, but Kelly used her implant to zoom in on the main entrance and saw a few aliens lingering around tables there, searching through the remaining name cards. "Donna must have been up all night arranging the seating," she said with grudging admiration. "I hope that she had help."

"I'm sure that Libby pitched in to tell her if any of the off-network aliens are currently at war," Joe said. He pulled out the closest chair at the head table for Kelly, and then slipped into the seat next to her with a groan of relief. "Maybe I will go see that Farling doctor tomorrow."

"Speaking of doctors, did you know that you were carrying around Woojin's contribution to Lynx's baby for the last two weeks? Apparently he's the oldest son in his generation, and his family made him freeze a sample before they let him join the military in his teens."

Joe's jaw dropped, and he stared at Kelly in surprise. "But when Wooj asked me to stop by that bank, I swear he said something about the family jewels."

"You men just can't talk about the important things in life without making jokes, can you?"

"Look who I found," Czeros said, approaching the head table with Gwendolyn in tow. Her friend looked so different from Kelly's memory that she wouldn't have recognized the clone if she had passed her in a corridor.

"Gwendolyn!" Kelly jumped up to hug her. "How long has it been? I didn't see you dancing."

"I'm too out-of-practice," the Gem replied. "I watched you and the children until the floor got so crowded that I couldn't see anything, and then I found a game of eight-handed Flonk going on in the card room and lost track of time."

"Is Mist still in stasis?" Kelly asked. "Dorothy is in the fashion business now and she's saving a spot for her."

"I'm sure that Mist will jump at the prospect when she wakes," Gwendolyn said, slipping into the seat next to Kelly.

Dring leaned in over Kelly's shoulder and whispered, "I have an award to present if you would join me at the lectern for a moment."

Kelly wanted to ask what it was about, but the Maker had already moved away, so she rose and followed him to the little raised platform with the speaker's stand at the center of the dais. Loud conversations in dozens of languages came to an abrupt halt when the guests saw that Dring intended to speak, and an eerie silence filled the giant hall.

"My friends," the Maker addressed the audience. "You've all danced and played hard, and I won't keep you from your supper any longer than necessary. We are gathered here today to honor the achievements of a diplomat who you may never have heard of from a species that some of you have yet to encounter. I have seen many civilizations come and go, and it is my fondest wish that the Humans prove to be more than a passing fad. I am presenting this award on behalf of my own species to the ambassador who restored our relations with the Stryx."

Dring reached into the interior of the lectern and brought out a hand-crafted trophy that reminded Kelly of something that her father had won at a fishing tournament back on Earth. Instead of a bass, it featured a thick golden book open on a pedestal, like the dictionary in the living room of her mother's home. There was a round of polite applause as the Maker handed over the award.

"Perhaps you could read the inscription for our guests?" Dring suggested.

Although she couldn't think of anything that would be more embarrassing, Kelly didn't see any way out of it, so she read out loud, "Best Human Ambassador to Union Station."

There was another smattering of applause, and a few wiseacres began crying "Speech! Speech!" and tapping their silverware on anything that would make noise.

Dring stepped down and returned to his place at the head table, gesturing for the Best Human Ambassador to Union Station to say something. Her implant pinged with a level-ten alert from the Galactic Free Press, only the second one she had received as a subscriber, but she couldn't afford the distraction and mentally waved it off.

"I'm speechless," Kelly began, and was immediately drowned out by a roar of approval from the guests, whose translation implants had taken the two words at face-value. As the ambassador moved away from the lectern to return to her seat, she caught a glimpse of her mother, who was sitting next to the EarthCent president at one of the nearby round tables. Marge was shaking her head in disbelief.

"I don't see why Dring had to be so specific about the inscription," Joe groused as his wife sat down. "You're the only human ambassador Union Station has ever had."

"You know he hates to offend anybody," Kelly said absently, still watching her mother's table where an active discussion was taking place among several of the guests. Then Chastity and Walter both rose from their seats, to a mixed chorus of boos and laughter from the humans present, and approached the head table.

"We want to apologize and to assure you that a correction has already been issued," Chastity told Kelly.

"It was just a bit of harmless fun, but the intern we left in charge of the newsroom made a small error in judgment," Walter added. "We'll make sure it's never repeated in the future."

"What are you talking about?" Kelly demanded, and then it occurred to her to check the level-ten alert on her heads-up display. The story featured a close up of Dring handing her the trophy, and the large caption read, "Ambassador Meets Maker." She snorted. "That's pretty clever."

"Read the story," Chastity urged her.

Kelly got through two sentences before she stopped and exclaimed, "But this is my obituary!"

"We keep them current for the famous humans on the tunnel network," Walter explained. "It's just that all of our staff is here tonight, and the intern misinterpreted my caption and triggered our emergency coverage protocol. It seems we have to rewrite those guidelines."

"Look on the bright side, Ambassador," Chastity said. "Everybody you know is here. By the way, my mom said to tell you that you're not in your assigned seat."

"We came in the back way, with Srythlan," Kelly explained. Chastity just shrugged and then returned to her own place, a chagrined-looking Walter in tow. The waitstaff of the Empire Convention Center, both biological and bot, flooded into the hall with serving trays.

"Hey, I ordered the chicken," Joe complained, pushing away a plate of barely congealed jelly. "What's this yellow glop?"

"Send it this way," an alien four seats to his left called.

Kelly looked down at her own plate and barely contained her gag reflex at the squirming pile of larvae. She rose to her feet and looked down the row of ambassadors to locate Crute, whose seat she had inadvertently taken. With any luck, the Dollnick ambassador would have her spaghetti.

"For you, Joe," Gwendolyn said, passing along a plate with chicken and green beans that had been delivered fire-brigade style down the long table.

"Thanks," Joe replied, accepting his supper from the clone. "It's still better than the service at that hotel we stayed at in Manhattan."

"You took the words out of my mouth," Kelly said, as she spied the Grenouthian ambassador returning a plate of spaghetti to a waiter. "There's no place like home."

EarthCent Ambassador Series:


Date Night on Union Station

Alien Night on Union Station

High Priest on Union Station

Spy Night on Union Station

Carnival on Union Station

Wanderers on Union Station

Vacation on Union Station

Guest Night on Union Station

Word Night on Union Station

Party Night on Union Station

Review Night on Union Station

Family Night on Union Station

Book Night on Union Station

LARP Night on Union Station

## About the Author

E. M. Foner lives in Northampton, MA with an imaginary German Shepherd who's been trained to bite bankers. The author welcomes reader comments at e_foner@yahoo.com.

You can sign up for new book announcements on the author's website - IfItBreaks.com

CPSIA information can be obtained
at www.ICGtesting.com
Printed in the USA
BVHW080016060222
628090BV00007B/605

9 781948 691123